I am Just Jes

ARTHUR H. BARNES

PUBLISHED BY FIDELI PUBLISHING INC.

ISBN: 978-1-60414-811-4

Fideli Publishing Inc.
119 W. Morgan St.
Martinsville, IN 46151

www.FideliPublishing.com

Cover art: Original painting by Pam Montoya

North Central Alabama circa 1831

"Hey, you big black nigger," the auctioneer yelled. "It's your turn. Get your black ass up on the platform and show off your big black muscles."

This was the fifth time Jes had endured such insults and it didn't bother him anymore. He had been shuffled from one plantation to another ever since he was old enough to draw attention.

When he was taken as a prisoner from his African home and family, he was about four years old. None of his relatives was captured at the same time in that group of slaves.

Now at the age of about eighteen — he wasn't sure exactly how old he was — he stood out above most of the blacks being sold at the slave auction. He couldn't remember much about Africa and coming to this crazy country called America, but somewhere way back in his very early childhood, someone, maybe his African mother, had impressed upon him the value of being proud.

Jes looked around at his present being and could not find any part of himself that he was not deeply proud of. His clothes may have been old and torn, covered in crudely sewn patches, but his hair wasn't too long and he was very clean. Even his toenails were clean and trimmed.

They held the auction at the village center of Woodville, Georgia where it would draw the biggest crowd of potential buyers.

As he took to the steps, he began to reflect on the different plantations where he'd become known as a trusted and hard-working field boss. He had made it his business to learn everything he could about farming, and growing the South's most needed crops. Cotton was the number one item, then tobacco and finally, corn. There were other lesser crops but they did not bring the badly needed monies that the major crops did.

Still, he, despite his meager education and inability to read or write, had mastered most of the science of soil and seeds.

By watching and asking many questions, he was able to gain a lot of information and knowledge about bugs and other insect problems and the most important turning of the fields.

He was a gentle soul, able to get along with most other field hands and the white bosses. The last plantation owner had fallen on hard times and now was selling his remaining important assets, his slaves.

Jes took his place on the platform, which was a makeshift wobbly bench of rough-cut timbers, full of mean, sharp splinters. The soles of his bare feet were like hard leather because shoes were something that he had never gotten used, and couldn't afford, anyway. Plus, they just got in his way when he was working.

Finding the smoothest place with the fewest splinter boards, he took off his ragged, sun-bleached shirt and dropped the bib of his many times washed bib overalls to expose his upper body to the crowd. He turned sideways so that he showed off his best feature, his perfect body. To give all the white folks a best look at his chest and arms muscles, he flexed as they vibrated and flashed in the hot sun. Some people even made kind comments. He was one proud colored man.

He looked to the right to see what kind of community he was in. The dirt street was no different from many he had seen, but the people seemed on the poor side with rough clothing and sloppy dress. At first glance, the poorly kept town was just another poor place, with wooden sidewalks made from bleached boards of old buildings. To his left, all he could see were a few regular-styled wooden buildings. A lone dog sat scratching its behind and that made Jes smile. "Dog," he whispered, "I knows just how you feel. Dey's warm sweat runnin' down my backside an I's wishin' I could scratch it."

He took a long look at the auctioneer to see just how mean he really was. The auctioneer was unshaven and had the usual big lump of tobacco in his left cheek, the dark swizzle of tobacco juice dripping down his chin.

The man had oiled Jes's upper body to make his muscles appear stronger and larger. It was a hot day and the sun glistened from the rivulets of sweat that ran down his body, making him stand out. As he turned to give all the white folks the best look, he deliberately flexed his arm and shoulder muscles. Several of the potential buyers gave a mumbled approval of this fine example of a strong, sturdy hard-working slave.

As he turned from one side to the other, there were cruel remarks being yelled at him from almost every white face that was staring up at him. At every twitch of his muscles, the auctioneer gave him a sharp jab to his ribs with a long stick. He grit his teeth against the pain and smiled back at them. *Go ahead you white bastards. I be a better farmer dan any of you. Weren't for all us black folks, y'all wouldn't have a pot to piss in.*

The auctioneer moved him to one side of the platform. His years as a slave had taught him how to be calm and stand quietly. He had impressed everyone beyond the hateful remarks. His muscles glistening along his dark body made him look more fit than any of the other slaves. Slowly, he looked over the potential buyers, wondering which one would be his new boss. From just the looks of them, not one impressed him as being a good plantation owner and farmer.

His eyes caught a face that was far back of the main group, standing under a large craggy oak tree. He couldn't stop looking at well-dressed man. *Now dat's a man who's somebody. Maybe he treat his slaves with some respect. I be proud if buy me.*

For some reason, he took great notice of the man's tanned face and the way he looked back. "Dat a man who know a great deal 'bout something. I wonder if he be wantin' a good slave."

He also noted that after a short while, the man stared back at him the same way he was staring at the man. After a few minutes, he noted that the man had walked away. He felt that maybe it would be much better to belong to such a well-dressed man and was emotionally disappointed.

After more than an hour, standing in the hot sun, there had been several low bids the auctioneer just laughed at.

The boss auctioneer stepped upon the platform and said, "Come with me." Then, in a very loud voice, "Come on, boy, someone has paid a great price to buy you and make you his nigger. Now, you get your black ass to that wagon over there." He pointed to the same wagon under the oak tree where Jes had noticed the differently dressed gentleman. "Don't ya say one word; if he wants ya to talk, he'll tell ya."

Jes was stood next to the wagon along with seven other people of color, two young pleasant-looking ladies and five older black men. Four well cared for horses were hitched to the passenger-type wagon.

His new owner directed him to sit on the seat beside him and immediately said, "I am Mr. Loving and just who or what are you called?"

"Dis goin' ta be dif'rent," Jes said to himself and climbed up to the seat where he had been directed.

After Jes was secured on the seat, his new owner handed him the reins and said, "You do know how to handle a team of fine horses don't you?"

Jes was so surprised, that he fumbled with the eight straps that controlled the animals.

"Now let's get on the road for we do not have all day," Mr. Loving said. "In fact, it's a day and a half to my ranch that people around here call a plantation."

It was the first time Jes noted Mr. Loving's different way of speaking.

Looking down at his naked feet that had never known shoes, Jes was embarrassed by their callused appearance. Never in his still young life had he paid any serious attention to his personal look. He had made sure that at all times he was clean but often time a little ragged, with the only clothes that he could afford, the same worn threads he had been wearing for years. Now, with his new owner addressing him as a "Mister" for some reason, that issue seemed important. His feet had spread out to a width so that only a shoemaker could fit his over- sized feet. He made a mental note to at least wash them and maybe in time, find some shoes that would serve the purpose.

They had traveled several miles when Mr. Loving stated that he was from a far away place called England. All his life he wanted to be a great farmer and work the soil, put seeds in the ground, grow fine crops, and live a peaceful life.

"My name is Richard Loving and I come from a very wealthy family that was famous in the coal industry in England. I found that getting all dirty from coal dust wasn't so bad but I wanted to see my labors return more than black rocks and lung disease. I searched all over the southern part of America and finally found this out-of-the-way hamlet with good soil and bought what I think will be my dreamland. All I ever wanted to do was be a good gardener and grow the finest items I could. Now just what is your name, Mr. black man?"

Now, he was in a real quandary. He had never been spoken to as a "mister" and hesitated for a long time.

"You do speak?" asked Mr. Loving.

Slowly, choosing his meager English words very cautiously, "If I knows how ta spell it right, it's jus plain J-e-s. I's also got da name Henry for my final name." Again, he waited, choosing more words just as carefully. "Da first came ta me from da cap'in of da ship dat brung me here. When da crew badger me, I be on da open parts of da ship an dat's when da cap'in tole his men not ta bother me. He say, 'Jes leave da kid lone.' Dat's how I figure I got named.

"I tink my final name be 'cause of da owner when I first come ta be a slave. His last name Henry. I doesn't know or 'member my name afore. Dat's 'bout all I 'member right now, Mr. Lovin'."

For many moments, there was no sound but the clink of the horses' hooves and the grinding of the wagon wheels as they bounced over the rough rocky road. Jes noticed the look of approval on Mr. Loving's face as he pulled the horses over to a creek to let them drink. He let the animals drink their fill, then guided them on the way.

The sun was getting low in the west when Mr. Loving announced he had arranged for them to camp alongside a creek that was situated on a friend's plantation. As they neared the destination for the night, Mr. Loving informed them they would make a quick camp and all would have a good supper and maybe get better acquainted.

"I enjoy sleeping out under the night as much as I can. Will that be alright with each of you?"

It seemed very strange that their new owner asked them for their approval of almost everything.

Each of Mr. Loving's newly acquired slaves just looked at each other, no doubt wondering just what kind of slave owner this man was.

After another hour of bouncing over some very rough ruts and large holes in the road, Mr. Loving directed Jes to turn to their right at the next road. Some newly plowed fields, sent their clean fresh, earthy smell to greet them as they meandered along the ruts of the road. The newly turned ground made Jes feel content.

"Maybe dis Mr. Lovin' be da bes' owner I eber has," he whispered to himself.

As Mr. Loving had stated, a slow stream ran through the meadow that was to be their camp for the night.

"Mr. Lovin', whar do y'all want ta make camp?" Jes asked.

There was a slight rise alongside a deeper pool. He pointed, directing Jes to set the wagon at a level place, then directed several of the other black men to gather some dry firewood so that they could have a nice quiet dinner.

Jes unhitched the horses and gave them a chance to drink. Jes took a long drink of the cold, sweet fresh water. He patted each horse on the nose and neck, talking gently to them, assuring he would always take good care of them.

"You's are the finest animals dat I has eber seen." He then chose the best grass nearby and tethered them for the night.

None of the slaves noticed that Mr. Loving had placed two large covered boxes under canvas in the back of the wagon. He asked two other men who were at the back to please unload the boxes. For any slave to be asked "please" was unheard of. They sensed that there was something very different in their future and a good feeling of long gone happiness slightly returned.

With the two boxes opened, the aroma revealed the makings of a good meal. There was a large, fully cooked smoked cured ham and some already roasted large sweet potatoes wrapped in thick brown paper, along with a pile of fresh-picked sweet corn still in the outer husk.

Mr. Loving asked, "Do either of you ladies know how to cook over an open fire?"

To be addressed as ladies was another new experience for the women.

"We'll need to put the potatoes and the corn over some hot coals and might need to boil some water for coffee. Can you do that?"

Mr. Loving then explained that when he left his ranch he had his hands prepare a special long-lasting, slow-smoked ham. That, along with already cooked sweet potatoes, tightly wrapped in paper for long keeping, would be their dinner.

His use of the word "hands" for his other farm workers did not go unnoticed by all the new colored people in the group.

The corn was still in its green shucks and would be placed over a bed of coals, turned often, until it was cooked just right. The sweet potatoes were unwrapped and piled over some almost dead coals just long enough to heat through.

"How many what you called hans does you has, Mr. Lovin'?" The tone of Jes's question caused Mr. Loving to hesitate for a few moments.

"Mr. Jes, I do not like the word slave and therefore prefer hands that work for me. It's disrespectful to call them anything but what they are, working hands." He hesitated for several seconds. "I've owned so many acres for just over four years and find that thirty-one men and women just cannot do all that I want and need them to do. They work real hard with the farming and keeping some of the things in reasonable repair. There is a lot that I want to do and that's why I acquired all of you fine-looking people. My new hands.

A shock sped down Jes's spine. At no time and nowhere had he been addressed as "mister." He waited for any other comments that Mr. Loving might make.

Both of the colored girls took steps toward Mr. Loving and almost in harmony said, "Yas master, we both knows how to cook and in any place. Jus show's us where the cooking tools be and we's both will get to work."

All of the new hands took full notice of Mr. Loving when the girls called him "Master." Stepping very close, Mr. Loving asked all of them to gather around him.

"People, understand from this moment on, I am not your master. I am well aware of what the other plantation owners demand to be called by their slaves but I am not one of them. Where I came from, there is no such class of people and I do not like what and how the people of color are treated here. I will not be referred to by any name other than 'boss' or 'Mr. Loving.' Does each of you fully understand?"

In unison, they said, "Yes, Mr. Lovin'."

"Before we go any further, I want to know all your names. Jes has already given me his name. He pointed to the younger of the two women. "You first, please.

"Mr. Lovin', my onlyest name be Marty. Dat's da only one dat I's been called by."

The second girl instantly replied, "I's called Gloria an do not know where's I gots such a name."

Without saying another word, Mr. Loving looked at the men and with out hesitation the taller of the five men spoke up.

"I be Bones, an lookin' at my skinny body, I's not need ta 'splane."

The next four men simply said their names and did not go any farther.

"Now, that's good. It gets us off in great shape. All I have to do is remember them and to whom they belong. After we're settled at my farm, we'll get all of the names straight and talk about and how everyone will be treated. Now all of us need to get some of that good food in our bellies and settle in for the night."

The food soon disappeared and as the fire started to lose its glow, six of the blacks began to sing several of the old traditional black spirituals. Jes couldn't help but notice that one of the new colored men's voices was that of a deep beautiful bass tone and resonated throughout the evening marking the man as one to talk to. Jes learned that his name was Leroy.

The song went on, "Going to set down and rest a while, ain't going to grieve, my Lord, no more." There were no loud voices but they had a thankful sound to them.

Mr. Loving moved close to Jes and began to inquire about the history of the South.

"Mr. Lovin', I's don' really knows. I's not been here so long dat I knows such things. We's all try ta keep out of da slave owners and field boss's ways. Dey seem ta hate us colored folk. Y'all have us puzzled by yo' talk dat you is jus the boss. We ain't use ta such freedom. Do your last name, Lovin', has ta do wit you bein' kine ta all colored folk?"

Mr. Loving just smiled. He took out a well-used, twisted stem pipe and began to fill the large bowl. He made no effort to answer Jes's comment. Taking a stick with a lit end, he lit his pipe and took several long, deep draws of the burning tobacco. Folding his hands across his outstretched legs, he began.

"Mr. Jes, and everyone else, in England — do you know where England is on this earth? I needed to find a different way to feel good about just being alive and doing something that I feel is useful and good. All my people were coal mine owners. They go back in time many generations. Do you know what a generation is, Jes?"

Jes didn't answer.

"A long time ago," Mr. Loving continued, "some one hundred years or more, they found a small, high quality coal deposit and started their own mining company. As it developed further, it became one of the largest deposits of fine coal in all England. My family became very wealthy and joined the rich clubs, owning expensive horses, going on fox hunts and to grand parties. When I was about 22 years old, they tried to pressure me into a marriage with one of their friend's daughters. I wanted nothing to do with having a house full of crying kids and relatives, so I demanded to be on my own.

"I tried to work in the family office, counting pieces of paper, having tasteless lunches with people, listening to dull conversations with so-called friends. I couldn't continue. After several long and tiring years, I put most of my considerable money into a bank trust. Even now, as far away from England as I am, I get my part of the family profits. They must be large, for what is sent to my bank is more than many plantations make in a lifetime. I then sailed for this country that I had heard so much about. I brought only enough money that would let me purchase what I thought would be my final place. The rest is in a bank I don't have a name for my farm, it's just a farm.

"I had no idea of what I might find or do In North Carolina. I struck up a conversation with a tobacco merchant who convinced me to buy into the great profits of tobacco. As I learned about the crop, I also learned where and how it was grown. Farming had always been a hobby of mine so I began traveling through the southern states visiting some of the plantations. I searched all over the South until I found a place where I knew I'd be happy. I guess I found what I wanted, not a great plantation but one that I thought that I could manage and make the best. It has good soil and plenty of good water and I can watch the seeds grow into useful plants that can make money.

"There are two ridges of low hills that run from a place called Woodville to the south and slightly east. To the west is a much larger town, Huntsville. It seems to be the center of all the plantation business in the region. I've only visited both places to buy the foodstuffs, where one buys farming equipment and the other needed items.

"My farm is out of the nearest regular town called Woodville. It is some twelve miles in a small valley with just a no named hamlet called Spike. Spike is a self-built community of just white folk that have a special dislike for people, especially people of color. At the foot of the hills south, the land breaks out to very low rolling hills and very good farmland. There are no formal roads but a dirt two-rut lane that goes from Woodville, through Spike and past my farm and on to wherever, I don't know. There is a much-neglected plantation just across a stream that separates our lands. If one cares to, it will take them to the larger town of Huntsville. A very good stream separates my farm and a grumpy old plantation owner just to the south and over a wooden bridge.

"It took me another few years to find the property that pleased me. The owner didn't know much about fine farming and really, neither did I at the time. I made him a good offer of $8,000 for some sixteen hundred acres and he agreed. That's where we'll be tomorrow, your new home.

"And that's about it, Mr. Jes.

A New Home

Near noon of the second day, Mr. Loving directed Jes to take the next turn to their right.

"This is the beginning of my farm, and your new home. At the present time, I have some thirty other black men and three women, my keepers and great cookhouse attendees, keeping my meager crops and buildings in fair shape. I'm in hopes that by bringing the seven of you new people, I can make some improvements to both the farm fields and some better housing for all of you."

The smooth gravel road that led along a twisted roadway was lined by many old giant oak trees with long shaggy strands of gray moss hanging from what seemed like every limb. Jes thought what a beautiful picture, almost bringing him vague memories of Africa.

"Mr. Lovin'," Jes asked, "does you always keep yo' plantation ... well farm ... lookin' su' neat an clean?"

Jes's question caught Mr. Loving off guard. "Mr. Jes, I take great pride in everything I have. I feel that if one does not take the best care he can of that which he is responsible for, he should not have anything. That goes especially for any of the people who work for me and my animals and how they're cared for and treated. I noticed that you were talking to my horses, making them settled as they paced along the road, and that impressed me."

As they rode past the scattered shanties, Jes had a quick thought of the many such places that he had lived and wondered about Mr. Loving's comment, "Better housing for his working hands."

"Mr. Jes," Mr. Loving said, "I am in need of a main man to manage all the fieldwork and some of the buildings that I have. There's a great need for new housing for all the working folks. They now live in shanties like that don't even keep out nasty bugs or the cold of winter, and have poor places for preparing their food. Something has to be done, and soon.

"You've already impressed me as a man that thinks and gets things done the right way. I want you to be my manager of everything, especially the farm hands. Do you want to be my manager, Mr. Jes?"

Jes hesitated. "Mr. Lovin', mos' plantations has a white field boss an he usually mean. You sure you wants me ta be field boss? 'Cause I's not mean or cruel to anyone or anything."

"Mr. Jes, that's why I'm sure you're the best man, because I will not tolerate any mistreatment of my animals or the people who work for me. Right now, all the old shacks are open to the weather and lean every which way. There are mean bugs, and the cold months aren't too far away. Something needs to be done and soon so that all of you don't freeze to death. If I draw some plans for new housing, do you think with the help of all the other men, you can put them together?"

Jus what kind of slave owner has I become owned by? Jes rolled Mr. Loving's statement over several times in his mind. Such a request had to be well thought about before he dared to offer a sensible reply. With all that Mr. Loving was sharing with him, he didn't want to make any mistakes. "Mr. Lovin', y'all wan' me ta do a lot of da things 'round here. I needs ta learn all da dif'rent peoples and 'bout the fields and such. If'n ya wan', I can do all o'dat, an I promise ta do da bes' job I knows how. I can larn that what I don' know. So, yes'sa, I be yo' manager if dat be what you wants. I's nebber been boss afore, so I's guessin' it's time ta learn something new."

As they arrived at the farm, Mr. Loving pointed to the houses that all the colored lived in and apologized because they were so dilapidated, but must make do for the time being. "We are going to change all of them." As they passed the last colored cabin, Mr. Loving pointed it out by commenting, "See there, Mr. Jes, there are five of my workers living in that one decaying shack without any sanitation or any heat and means of disposing of their garbage. I cannot stand to see anyone living in such a poor way. Put that at the top of our list for things to get done."

A number of the older hands stood out to see just what kind of colored additions Mr. loving had brought. Some smiled and waved a friendly hand. One yelled, "You's gone like it jus fine here."

Jes quickly noted many of the fields were green with new crops. Small shoots of corn, some small acreage of tiny tobacco plants, were showing their first color of green, but Jes noticed the green wasn't shiny like it should be and made a mental note to ask why.

"Most of this season's crops have all been planted," Mr. Loving said, "and seem to be doing just fine. Now on to the important work the new houses.

"Mr. Lovin', I's done a heap of different woodwork over the past years, but mostly just growing crops. I's did some repair of the master's own houses and barns. I see no difference to maybe build'n a few new, and not so fancy, houses. I's pretty good with a sharp handsaw and don't hit my fingers more than once. If y'all wants ta put on paper the way yous wants ta make da new houses, I recon dat we do it. When you plan ta have us start?"

"I have most of the lumber already stacked near the horse barn. It may take me several days to draw up the working plans for at least two different types of houses — one for the single men and another for those who might have a wife or woman. Why don't we wait until we all meet the other workers, and by then you might have some idea of how the rooms should be made? So far, I have only three other women workers and they're somewhat living with men of their choice. I don't like to have couples on my farm that live together and aren't legally married. I also have two young colored ladies to keep house and do my cooking.

"The unmarried men and women often, well, there are children from that kind of relationship and I don't think the children should have to suffer from the lack of two parents. How do you feel about having a woman and not be married to her? I'm learning that many of the customs here are very different from what I was used to in England. I will have to trust all of you to keep me from making a big mistake in how you want to be treated. I also have a lot to learn."

Jes couldn't get to sleep. He had taken shelter in the harness building that Mr. Loving said was the first new construction he had done. The hard floor was very different to him and he found it difficult to get any sleep. A couple of blankets over fresh straw was much more satisfying. He wanted some sleep and snuggled down in the straw bed as far as he could.

The questions Mr. Loving had asked Jes caused a sort of whirling in his mind. As best as he could remember, he began to go back to the first time he was put to work as a slave. The word slave didn't mean much to him at his very young age, so he paid no attention to it. He'd been caught up with some of the black people he had traveled across that Ocean with and was considered part of the family.

He couldn't remember at what age he began to carry water to the plantation's slaves. He could barely remember that he was very young, working in the hot sun hoeing cotton or weeding the tobacco. Struggling with as much as he could think about, he managed to go back to his slave boss, who said, "Nigger boy, get your black ass on down the row of something that is growing and don't give me any sass." Jes was sure that with Mr. Loving, that would not ever happen again

There were several other plantations where he worked just like all the other slaves. As time went by, he became aggressively interested in what was being planted and the tending of the soil. It was an obsession with him and he constantly inquired, "Jus what dat for, and why is you doing all dat to the dirt?" He slowly learned the right way to turn the dirt to make it into rich healthy soil that would grow anything planted in it. Often he would see the white field bosses reading instructions for different crops and asked what they meant. "Nigger," they'd say, "you don't have any need to learn to read so just shut your black mouth and get back to work." It was always in a hateful tone but as usual, he just shrugged it off and went on with whatever he was doing.

The following day, Mr. Loving gave Jes a lone cabin all to himself.

It made him feel very separate from the other hands and he sought out one of the new men for a shared cabin. The new man's name was Leroy. Jes had more or less paid attention to Leroy when he first began the trip to Mr. Loving's ranch. He quickly learned that the new man was just as confused as he was about the way Mr. Loving treated his "hands."

Like Mr. Loving, Leroy stated his name by saying, "Mr. Jes," and before Leroy could utter another word, Jes firmly and with a good measure of authority said, "I be jus plain Jes. I ain't no mister."

Early the next morning, Mr. Loving met Jes.

"Mr. Jes, will you gather some of the other men and come with me? I want to show you how I built a very dry storage building for all my harnesses, saddles and other tack. It's a lot different than what I saw done by other storage places. The need is to have a very clean, dry place so that decay, mold and dirt cannot get into the storage area."

There was no just asking for several men, all of the farm hands simply began to follow the two men. They weren't about to be left out of any new means of a new type of building and further, they wanted to make sure that they didn't miss any of their new master's plan for them.

As they circled around several out buildings, Jes noted that some of them looked recently repaired and in very good condition. The main barn area was where the new storage place was located and it looked new as a bright penny.

As Mr. Loving opened the double doors, he pointed to the shiny floor. "This, gentlemen, is what I want to explain to all of you. It's called concrete and is hand made from mixing small rocks, sand and powdered cement. When properly mixed, it's poured into forms and let to dry. They are set exactly where the new floor is to be made. It's very easy to do and will not cause anyone any problems. I have all the material stacked under that black canvas over there. If you can help me beginning tomorrow morning, we'll start to set the floor of at least two, maybe three, of the new houses. I have enough plans to begin that part of the project.

"The new homes will be much warmer, there will be no cracks between the wall boards. From what I've seen of other slave houses, the floors are made from very rough plank wood and after just one hot summer, the boards shrink, letting in the cold, bugs and other varmints. I'd like to have clean water run through pipes to each house with a faucet close by so that no one has to carry water very far. I'm not sure that we can find the piping material even in the town of Huntsville. This is again something new to all of you. How many of you have ever seen or had fresh clean water right next to your homes? Each of you will have that type of home when we can get all the new buildings completed. Can you do such a floor?"

Jes had to inquire, "Mr. Lovin', jus where you learn all dat stuff?"

"Gentlemen, in England that is the way many of the more modern buildings are begun. After the cement has hardened, it's called concrete. It will last way past our time if we mix everything correctly." Mr. Loving went on to say they would have to level each house foundation with strong boards, build what were called forms to keep the wet stuff inside the exact position of the floor. "It's not hard but a little work is required. I can direct all of you in the proper way that it has to be done."

Other than a slight grunt of understanding and several groans, they made their way back to their respective homes.

Jes sat late in the hot evening, going over in his mind the comments that Mr. Loving had told all of them. I jus have ta stay close to dat man and I's might learn something. Hess the smartest white man I eber see.

The colored people had already made the decision to have one central eating place. They built a covered patio-like shelter with rough tables made of old boards and benches for chairs. The floor was hard packed clay. The outer wall that faced into the wind was boarded up so that if there was a storm, they could at least eat in comfort. The women and two of the older men had decided to be the regular cooks and were excused early from fieldwork in order to fix each evenings meal. The cooking was done over a large fire pit that had an iron grate over the pit to hold cooking pots. A stone oven had been built so that they could have good loves of fresh bread.

Dinner was the most food and usually made around some pork that had been smoked or a freshly slaughtered pig. In all cases, the pig had been split in half and roasted over an open spit that cooked the whole side in one afternoon. Coals had to be added as the fire diminished. One of the men would be excused from fieldwork to make sure that the fire didn't go out. The cook took great pride in having the best-cooked pork for the evening meal. There was enough meat left over for lunch the next day if anyone cared to make a lunch. Sliced slabs of bread with a cut of the cold pork was usually the only food for a lunch.

Breakfast was usually left up to the individual person from leftovers from the previous evening meal. Jes had selected a small table that was at one side so that he could study each person to learn about their individual habits. "I gots ta know all they names."

He chose Rube first because Rube had made an effort to get to know Jes. Rube sat down without being asked.

"Mr. Jes, I's been here from the very beginning when Mr. Lovin' took over the plantation. Dat was with da owner before Mr. Lovin'. I's was just a slave 'til Mr. Lovin' gots all us an laid down he law. He say dere be no one callin' a person slave or nigger." Rube said the words with hate blended in. "He say he either Mr. Lovin' or 'da boss'. Now, I hear him say dat you be da new field manager. Dat's not da way we's used ta doin' we always being told how and when ta do. You gonna treat us da same as dem?"

"Mr. Rube, I nebber be treated so friendly an I don' wan' ta be treated any dif'rent. I is jus' a hand, same as you an the res' o'em. I call you dat 'cause you is the most smart colored man I see here so far. You jus' as Mr. Lovin' say, a ranch han, an I not be changin' dat. Dat be so fore-eber — a han dat work for Mr. Lovin'. He say he wan' me ta run da ranch just' as I wants, so I has lots ta learn. I won' be treatin' y'all any worse dan I's treated. We has a lot ta do an I want ta talk ta each man an woman by theirselfs, jus' like I's doin' ta you. Tell 'em ta come in one at a time ta sit wit me an talk."

All the rest of the evening, Jes sat with each one of the workers, asking them about their past slavery on different plantations and how they were treated before Mr. Loving acquired the ranch.

It was well past midnight when he saw that most of the hands were still present and asleep where they sat. He began to feel the strain of the evening. He stood up and addressed them. "Folks, my new friends, I apologize for keepin' ya up so late. I's know dat tomorrow be a hard day an y'all need ta rest."

Jes had slaughtered many different animals for other slave owners and was caught up in the way his new farm hands were going about dress-ing out a young porker. The animal weighed about 190 pounds. When it stopped hollering, they immediately put it into a large scalding kettle where hot water was all but boiling. When it was completely scalded, the hair was shaved from every inch of the animal with sharp knives. The skinned, naked carcass was then cut it lengthwise from head to tail, keeping the back part attached with the tough skin.

As he watched, they skewered it between two metal poles and sprinkled it all over it with spices before setting it over an open fire for cooking. It was beginning to flavor the evening air with a hungry sense of wanting to eat. The meat would be ready in about four hours for a massive late evening dinner. As it roasted, two men would turn the cooking pig on its other side several times.

Jes just stood and stared at the now roasting pig as it turned over the spit.

"I nebber saw a whole pig cooked dat way," he said to the closest man. "On all dem udder plantations, the masser only gib da head an sometime da feets for da colored folk. How come you cooking da whole ting?"

The man gave a broad smile. "We do da same 'til Mr. Lovin' be our boss. When we kill da firs' pig, when he ask, we cuts off da head an he told us da whole pig be foe us. He said dat as long as he was da boss, the hans get da whole pig an dat's da way it be eber since. Now hep me turn it afore it burn."

Jes remembered back to his early days as a boy when the plantation owner provided food for his slaves. When an animal was slaughtered for food, the worst parts were given to slaves as tokens of the owner's grace — the head, knuckles and bony parts, plus all the insides of the animals. That was just the way it was on every plantation, until he was bought by a plantation owner by the name of Mr. Parker. He shared all the animals and made sure that his slaves were well treated. Mr. Parker often said that nobody could do good work unless he or she was well cared for.

Almost all plantation owners thought that their slaves were valuable property with most treating the slaves by beating them for no reason, just sport, and laughing as they tore the skin off their backs.

A number of the ladies were busy with such items as sweet potatoes, roasted in low coals, and corn on the cob boiled in the large cooking pot. One of the men was a baker and had made big yeast loaves of bread for everyone even for breakfast tomorrow. Jes whispered to himself, "It's going to be a grand evening."

The evening was about dark when there was a loud noise of someone banging on a heavy tin pan announcing that dinner was being served.

Mr. Loving must have heard the noise also for he came strolling into the group softly saying, "Good evening all, and just where do you want me to sit?"

To everyone's delight, Mr. Loving strongly stated that the dinner was the very best that he had ever tasted.

There was one more surprise. Three of the ladies came out of one of the old houses with large pies in each hand. Jes knew what they were but said nothing. He wanted to see how Mr. Loving might react to what he imagined the boss had never tasted - sweet potato pie. As all expected he asked for a second helping and repeated his comment about all the food.

As the evening came to a close, most of the colored hands gathered around the still glowing fire and began to sing their spiritual songs. Jes and Mr. Loving sat back and reveled in the great harmony and beautiful song, "Peace in The Valley."

"There will be peace in the valley for me some day,

There will be peace in the valley for me Oh lord I pray!

There'll be no sadness, no sorrow, no trouble I see

There will be peace in the valley for me!"

Jes noticed Mr. Loving had a smile on his face. He knew that Mr. Loving was very aware of the struggle of all the colored people. Jes couldn't hold back the tears that slowly flowed down his cheek. For the first time being in a new country, he felt almost free.

He'd been so caught up with meeting his new colored friends that he didn't notice a single lit lamp hanging from one corner of the last shanty of a colored house. Pulling Rube aside, Jes asked, "What do dat lamp do? I nebber saw a lamp hanging lit for a house afore. Do it mean something?"

Rube said he was responsible for the lamp and had to make sure that it was lit every evening. "We don' really talk 'bout dat." For any opportunity for a man to talk was a real challenge. Given any excuse to speak and the words just flew.

Jes persisted. "Mr. Lovin' made me manager of da ranch an I's goin' ta make sure dat I's know what goes on here. So, answer me."

Rube slumped down and reluctantly admitted he was the only one who took care of the lamp. "'Fore Mr. Lovin' bought da plantation, da slaves try ta escape ta da north and be free. Dere's many o'both color an white folk dat tries ta hep. Da lamp show we one of da safe places dat escapin' slaves can come ta git shelter an eats, plus a goot frien'. We hides 'em out back in da deep woods. Mr. Lovin' have 'bout a hun'rud acre of wood on da back of he farm. Mr. Lovin' find out wha we doin' an 'bout scare da devil out o'us. He roun' all us up an we tole him all 'bout it. Few day later, he get da men folk an some board and make a shelter deeper dan da one we have. We make anober shelter out in da gov'ment wood.

"Now when a slave be tryin' ta get up North, dey see a lamp hangin' from da las' buildin' of da farm. Da color folk an sometime da white folk make sure dey has a safe place ta rest. Dey don' stay much more'n one night an go on da nex' day. Dey's many such hep 'long da way, like here. 'Bout a dozen a week pass by an we is proud ta hep. Do dat make ya upset?

"Some folk call dis a railroad. I nebber see a railroad jus' fa color folk but I's really happy dat one is passin by."

Jes had never heard of such a way for slaves to leave the bounds of a plantation and slave owner. He had to sit down for it was a lot of new information to think about and not make any mistakes. This was a very important service and he had to be a part of it.

"No, it don' make me upset," expressed Jes, "I jus wan' ta know when dey come. I hep wit showin' dem da restin' place and mayhap wit food. Rube, if we is goin' ta build some cabins, we needs ta fine out what's in dem cabins now. How 'bout you show me some of dem old cabins so's I can be tellin' Mr. Lovin' what we needs."

Rube wasn't one to linger when there was something new going to happen, so he stood up and asked Jes if he wanted to do it now. Jes was a little surprised because of the late evening hour but joined Rube as he explained that the oldest cabin was the farthest one and it was about to fall down all by itself.

As they passed three of the other shanty-looking cabins, Rube explained about how bad their condition was, but still used by the hands.

"I sure likes da way Mr. Lovin' makin' life here on dis ranch a better place ta live dam where's I been at afore. Dem new cabins be makin' da hans real happy an they workin' eben harder." Rube pointed at one of the cabins. "Dat's da worse of da whole lot. You's see it rottin' from da groun' up an it lean ta one side. If da wind kick up, it be comin' down all by itself."

As Jes and Rube stepped onto the almost rotten deck boards, they heard a sound that cautioned them that the deck might collapse at any moment. The screen door was void of any screen, with pieces of the old screen still hanging from the broken frame. The door frame was ready to drop. It was hanging from what looked like old harness leather used as hinges and one of the leather hinges was already decayed to two separate pieces.

They entered a darkened room that was obviously the kitchen, eating space and occupants' place to get together. The flooring was almost as bad as the porch decking. Each board had a gap between it and the next board large enough to put a finger through the space. Any number of bugs or small critters could easily enter the house at will.

Jes quickly estimated the size of the whole building and came up with four rooms that seemed to equally divide the interior space. He figured the whole house was about eighteen by sixteen feet. A room that Rube commented about was supposed to be a front room but every house used it as another bedroom. If there were only a man and a woman living in the house, there were two rooms that allowed for two other people to share.

As both men surveyed the cabin, Jes took special note of the meager furnishings. There was a cast-iron cook stove that might accommodate two cooking pots at a time and a firebox and shelf for keeping food warm. The stove sat on a layer of flat stones to keep any stray sparks of still-burning coals from setting the cabin on fire. There was also one very rickety table that was supposed to be for serving meals. All the flooring had large cracks that let in the cold and any critters that wanted some kind of shelter. All of the single cabins were not any different than most of what Jes had seen in all his years.

"Jus hope Mr. Lovin' have some better plans for da new cabins."

The two men stepped out the back door and were greeted by another series of steps. They were in worse condition than the front steps were. Off the edge of the rickety porch was what an insane person might call a bench; it was a joke that Jes thought was one of the colored hands attempt to add what could be considered humor.

Jes took the last step or what might have once been the last step. It was just crumbled, scattered boards that had once been a step, destroyed by hungry termites. He stumbled around trying to keep from falling to the ground. Recovering, he noticed that there was a string of well-kept gardens.

"Jus who keeps such fine gardens?"

"Whoever's libs in dat cabin does they own plantin'," Rube said, "an dey can keep or sell what dey grows to anyone. Mr. Lovin's house lady usually take all the dat grows. It mean dat Mr. Lovin' have fresh greens most times an he pay for dem 'bout the same as in any store. Dey's always better dan any store vegetables.

"Now dat pile of boards what's known as da outhouse toilet an be used when it ain't no other choice."

Jes had a smile as big as a house on his face for none of the other plantations would pay for anything. A broken pile of boards was supposed to be a bench. If one would try to sit on it, he would wind up in a pile of broken boards that were well chewed on thanks to the ever-present termites. On a staggered, weed-infested path was the outhouse. It was in no better condition than any other part of the house or porch.

Jes thought for a moment before he spoke. "If'n dis be what all da cabins be like, I guess we has lots of buildin' to do. Be takin' lot of time an people power, too. I guess dat I has a lot of talking to do with Mr. Lovin'. You sure dat all da cabins be no better dan dis one?" Jes, with his head low, began to recount the many problems with the new houses.

He stumbled along until he reached the other hands. Some of them noticed Jes's troubled face. One finally piped up and asked him, "Jus da trouble be, Mr. Jes? Y'all look downhearted. Don' dis farm an not bein' called slave make ya happy?"

Jes looked up to see just who had noticed his strained appearance.

"No Cal. I's jus taked a look at da living quarters an it done made me sick. It's goin' ta be lots o'hard work. I's got ta has a long talk with Mr. Lovin'." Jes began to walk toward the main house and Mr. Loving, with a lot of questions.

Serious Work

Daylight hadn't shown its warming face before Jes had most of the men lined up and telling them that today, with the crops all planted, they were going to start building their new homes. He assigned a job for each man to carry the wood for the forms and smaller stakes to keep the forms set in place.

It took all the colored men a total of four days to set the forms of just three houses. Mr. Loving was nearby to show and give instruction of each step. Mr. Loving had a set of plans for each hand's house. Jes was surprised at the added space of each home.

Jes asked many detailed questions as the work progressed. He thought that Mr. Loving might get tired of so many questions, so he hesitated to ask some of them, hoping in time, he could figure them out himself. Next, he asked Mr. Loving, 'Does you has some good hammers an handsaws? Buildin' be hard if we'don' have some real nice tool."

Mr. Loving smiled and told Jes to look in the large box at the back of the shed. As the other men lifted the lid, they all whistled.

"Dang, Jes, they's a lots o'bran' new tools! Dey's like dey's nebber be used. Saws an a pile o'hambers. I cain't waits ta gets my hans on dem an show jus what I can do."

Jes looked into the box and exclaimed, "Mr. Lovin', what we cain't make with such tools!"

As each floor dried, Jes began to direct the setting in place of the outside walls. It took a full month to have all the outside structures done and ready for the glass windows. Each board that was covering the outer wall was nailed together with a narrower board so that no bugs or wind would ever get inside the house. Mr. Loving had ordered all the glass windows he thought would be needed. They were another item that not many colored had enjoyed. In the past, a sheet or maybe less, a rag drape was hung where the window was located. As each house was finished, the three married couples with the few children moved in first. Next were the single men. All but Jes, who was given the last house. Each house had a small sitting room, a good size bedroom that two double beds would fit close and a kitchen that was small but very serviceable for a small family.

Mr. Loving and Jes couldn't find any of the pipes they needed to carry the clean water to the homes. They set one water supply between two houses and they had to share.

Calvin had shown that he could make almost anything and had started making a strong table for each new house. The chairs would have to wait for later

Jes and one other man began to take inventory of the tools and noted that Mr. Loving had even obtained a small barrel of large nails, just the right size for the larger structures.

"Mr. Lovin', you's forgot da mos' 'portant buildin' — da outhouse! We not doin' without dat."

Mr. Loving quickly added, "We will get to that as soon as we can. Maybe you can get several of the hands to select that best place and have them begin to dig the proper holes. Just how many outhouses do you think you'll need?"

Jes scratched his head and made several crazy faces before be could answer. "I tink dat if we has one outhouse foe two houses, dey share an has no problem. Oh well, dat's my job if Mr. Lovin' really make me boss of da hands."

Early the next morning, just as Jes had finished his breakfast, Mr. Loving came whistling from his house and in a loud voice proclaimed, "Jes, what a great morning to begin putting the frames in place for the new homes."

By the end of the first day, They had the outside walls set for all three houses. Mr. Loving decided that he had also better explain just how the walls had to be so and so.

It looked like a real circus. As many of the men that there was room for began to carry the different boards so Mr. Loving could direct how they would be put in place for walls. Not being familiar with the long boards, they would just grab a board, shoulder it and start to walk, often not watching the ends of the boards, hitting each other with them. A few angry words were uttered

Mr. Loving was well aware that it was the mid-season for planting the main crops, which had been done, and asked Jes if the two of them could walk the fields that had already been plowed. Jes was eager to get to his main interest of farming — that was his love.

"I sure does, Mr. Lovin'. I's jus wonderin' when ya might say someting 'bout getting' on wit da las' of da plantin'. We's already done da tabacky, and we late foe da cotton. Da corn 'bout knee high an look jus' fine."

Mr. Loving led Jes behind the barn to the field where tobacco had always been planted. Jes reached down, gathered a handful of the dark looking soil from the newly plowed acres, and brought it to his nose.

"Mr. Lovin', dis soil smell like sour milk. I don' tink it be a good place ta do tabacky or much else." He passed the soil to Mr. Loving so he could smell it.

"I never heard of anyone that could tell if a soil was good or bad by just smelling. How do you know that?"

Jes placed a very small amount of soil to his tongue. "Dat's ebben worse," he exclaimed.

Jes explained it had to be from the last time it was plowed. The remains from the last harvest must have been half-rotten when it was put under and it didn't turn to compost, as it should have. He suggested they plow the entire field under and let it just sit in the hot sun for maybe a month. The sour stuff would dry out and a new but different type of crop could be successfully planted.

"I's think's maybe corn would be a good next crop."

Mr. Loving didn't hesitate. "Jes if that's your advice, do it. I have a lot to learn from someone that knows just the right thing to do."

Jes stopped and looked down at his feet. Mr. Loving had convinced Jes that he should wear shoes. Jes had never had anything on his feet before and they were sort of wide and the soles as hard and tough as old harness leather. On the first trip into Huntsville, the only market, they had to search every shoe store to find the size that would fit and not wear blisters on his feet. They had to give up and selected a boot maker shop for some hand-made shoes. The boot maker told them he had made several pairs for slaves with extra large feet and they seemed to be fine.

Now, Jes looked at his shoes, and the soft soil brought back fond memories of walking through newly plowed fields. The fresh turned soil, squeezed between his toes told him that everything was great for the seeds, whatever was to be planted.

They then walked to the far back of Mr. Loving's property where a field had been made ready for a new seeding. Kicking the ground, Jes commented that the soil here looked real fine. "Mr. Lovin', what you plan to plant here?"

"We have a number of fine horses and good mules, they need good hay all year long so I asked the older hands to maybe plant the hay here. It's the furthest away from all the hard working crops and would be easier to take care of. As you already know, I treat my animals with a great deal of affection. Any reason that we might consider something else?"

It was then that Jes remembered the farm's working animals. The mules and horses had to be some of the best or Mr. Loving would not have had them. Excusing himself, Jes slipped away to the animal barn. As he checked each mule, he talked to it just as he would speak to any of the hands. "Hey mulie, you looks like yous being well cared for. Your outside look nice an bright, shiny all over. Yous must do good work." He went to all the mules.

As he came to the last one, the mule laid her ears back as though to bite, or any other harmful thing that she might do.

"Now why you so uppity and riled? Off your feed or jus tired? Maybe you been workin' too hard? I tink dat I be callin' you Grumpy 'cause you seems all bunched up an in a bad mood." Jes knew from long experience that most mules were always unpredictable and bad tempered.

Then Jes spotted the two fine horses that had pulled their wagon from the auction back to Mr. Loving's ranch. As he reached out to rub the nearest horse on the nose, it bent its head down so that Jes could reach it. As Jes brushed and patted him behind his ears, the horse, in a good-natured way, curled its lip and made a pleasing gesture. Jes asked, "So you 'member me at da auction. I greet ya foe da firs' time an you make me feel good dat I has such nice animals ta work wit. I wants ta' thank ya foe bein' so frien'ly." Da other horse make da same gesture ta Jes.

Mr. Loving had slipped into the barn and was watching Jes as he addressed all the animals. "Mr. Jes," he said, "I knew I was right when I asked you to be my ranch manager. The way you have begun to meet all my hands and just now, the farm animals, assures me that I have nothing to worry about. Look on the other side of the barn and you'll find a young, beautiful mule that needs training. She's yours and I know she will be your friend forever."

Jes quietly peeked behind the separations of the area. He was startled at the friendly looking young animal. He wanted to climb over the stall wall and put his arm around the wonderful little mule but he also knew that Mr. Loving was trying to survey all the fields for planting, which was now behind the best time for sowing seeds. As Jes left his new friend, he told her that he would be back soon and that they would get better acquainted. He hurried to catch up with Mr. Loving.

"We needs ta get da las' seed in da groun' soon or we's won' has a crop. Da hay will be jus' fine an I does like animals 'bout as much as anyone. I needs ta look at all da work animals an make sure dat they's bein' care foe. I's hope dat ya don' mine me bein' friendly wit da workin' animals, it's jus' how I be, Mr. Lovin'."

The two men walked all the remaining fields and did not change any of the plans for planting. They carried on a general conversation as they strolled through the fields. They came to the tobacco barn that appeared to have been older than some of the dirt. It leaned in several directions with many of the outside boards missing.

Jes just stood and stared. "Mr. Lovin', that won' do if'n ya wants ta cure da bes' tabacky in da couny. Has you thought 'bout rebuildin' da barn or mayhap makin' a new'un?"

Mr. Loving had a massive grin on his face and stated that he had saved the barn for last. "Jes, I've already ordered wood for a bigger and better barn but I don't know that much about what a curing tobacco barn should be like. Can you help me design one?

"Let's get to the house and we can put pencil to paper and come up with the proper curing barn, better than any in the county."

"Wait jus a minute Mr. Lovin'. We need ta study dat ole barn an see what's wrong wit it beside bein' ole an fallin' down. See da doe up dare? Dey's ways ta measure da coolin' an fresh air comin' in da barn so dat da tabacky won' dry over much. Dees ole doe be so rottey dey jus' barely holdin' onta da barn.

"Good tabacky gots ta has some mois'ure lef' in it or it jus' useless. They's some larger doe at da boddom, all jus' foe air gettin' ta da tabacky. It kinda a art ta make fine tabacky dat bring da bes' price.

"Dat smell ya smell be old rottey tabacky, 'cause da barn not be cleaned right. One ting foe shore, if da tabacky be da bes' kine, it need ta be cure in a clean place. We needs ta 'member dat ebber time we sells our tabacky. When ya git da wood foe da new barn?"

"Mayhap we need be goin' over da wood you has to see if we has da right thins. Ya seems ta be real good at makin' a record o'thins, likeya done wit da new houses for the hans. There be lots of har'workin' makin' a curin' barn. First we has ta git da tabacky plants in da groun', an soon."

Jes stepped off one side of what he thought the barn should be. "Mr. Lovin', dis should be da eas' wall foe dat's da way da coolin' air come from." He looked around until he found several stakes that he could use as markers for the corners. He finished his walking then asked Mr. Loving to go over the area with him. "Dat's 'bout da size we thinnin' 'bout. It make enough room foe da mos' tabacky we grow. What does ya tink 'bout dat, Mr. Lovin'?"

They sat for all the rest of the afternoon drawing many different ideas of what the curing barn would be like. Each time Mr. Loving described his thoughts, Jes would say, "Why you want dat?" or "Dat won' do, Mr. Lovin'."

As dark was setting in, the two housemaids came in and addressed Mr. Loving. "If you be ready, we has dinner to be served."

Jes stood up to leave when Mr. Loving let him know that he had planned to have Jes share his evening meal with him.

"After we eat," Mr. Loving said, "we can continue to finish the barn plans. I want to get all the supplies real soon."

Jes noted that Mr. Loving was fidgeting around something on his mind but hesitated to inquire. Finally, he could take it no longer because Mr. Loving had mentioned that he very much disliked not knowing the facts and potential problems that were just around the corner.

Taking a deep breath Jes began. "Mr. Lovin', yous seem ta be disturb. If I done somethin' wrong, I needs ta know it. Jus' like y'all, I hates ta be sittin' in da dark."

Mr. Loving must have anticipated such a question for he spoke out immediately.

"Jes, my friend, I have worked with many men, especially in the coal business. Most had a reasonable education about many things like horse shoeing, smelter work, and of course mining and building and such. I liked almost all of them for their many abilities. Now I've met and found a poorly educated black man that has shown me more caring and gentleness about people and farming than I thought I would ever know. I've tried to find the right words that wouldn't embarrass you or me. I don't know how to tell you how much you mean to me as a true friend and advisor. As I have already told you, when you know that something needs to be done — do it. Just tell me about what you're up to so that I won't feel so stupid if asked. Does that answer your concern about me?"

Quickly, Jes returned to the subject of a new barn. "'Bout how long does ya tink it will take ta make da barn? 'Bout da same time as win da tabaky ready ta harvest? Da workers cain't be doin' nothin' but workin' on da barn, 'cause dey needs ta be in da field. We bes' work on the barn af'er we's done in da field. Saturday an Sunday after all da color folk done they prayin' in da church, I do mo' work."

Mr. Loving frowned as Jes mentioned church. "Just where do the coloreds go to church?"

Jes hadn't considered his fellow man's belief in God. He himself had a deep and positive feeling about God but he had known for many years that his God was in his heart.

"Mr. Lovin', I is sorry ta say I don' know. Dey seems ta fine any place ta bend down on dey knees an say they prayer. Mostly, dey prays 'bout bein' a slave an bein' traded from they African homes an family. I be a God-fearin' mans, but I knows in my heart what I believes an dat don' scare me any. I be talkin' wit all of dem an see if dey like ta have a place foe church. I be doin' dat this evenin'."

After a few moments, Jes asked, "Mr. Lovin', time's a runnin' out foe some of da best crops, like cotton. It need ta get in da groun'. I knows they's several type of seed. Has ya thought on which ya want ta plant?"

Mr. Loving informed Jes that he was well aware of the best cotton type that if it was planted right and cared for, would bring the best dollars. "Let's go into the town where I do most of my trading and ask the man that buys only the best. We should start in the morning, it's an all-day ride there and back."

Jes had never traveled to the town before and was excited to see some other people of color and how they got along with the white folks.

That evening, Jes remembered that he had to ask all the hands about their religion and just where they found a church, or place that gave them the feeling of a church. He was puzzled when they explained that any place was God's place, but mostly, under a giant oak tree behind the barn. They said that the tree to them represented the strength of God and his promises.

"Now, 'bout the other slave plantations. Dey's 'bout da same," Jes said to Mr. Loving the following day. "Da plantation owners, dey has a field boss dat have a stick wit' leather straps tied ta it. Da leas' little ting dat bother da field boss, he bring painful, blood-lettin' hurts 'cross da slave backs. Even da women suffer da anger o'such men. Mose time, if'n da woman decent lookin', she keep da field boss an even da owner bed warm. Mr. Lovin', I does not understan' how one human person treat a person so cruel — even if they's a dif'ren' color. I jus' does not understand white folk at all."

Mr. Loving had no response but the look on his face let Jes know that he also didn't understand the slave owners' cruel ways toward any man, regardless of color. For a long time, no words were spoken between the two men. Then out of nowhere, Mr. Loving stated, "In my England, any one who treated another person that way was put in the dungeon for a long time. Do you know what a dungeon is Mr. Jes?"

Jes's simple reply, "No'sa, boss. I nebber hear dat word afore, but it soun' bad."

Late 1834

As they came to the town that Mr. Loving was familiar with, he told Jes it was Woodville and was in the county of Jackson, Alabama. "I'm not sure if you knew that Jes. Our little 'white only' hamlet of Spikes is in Marion County, Alabama, and is not even considered a town. The white people here aren't cast in the same ugly way as the whites in Spikes. It's difficult to understand how and why just a few miles from each other; the people are like from a different world. I guess that's just the way it is,"

The first stop was at a large market place where Mr. Loving spoke to the manager and left a long list of items that he would pick up as they left the town.

Mr. Loving then let Jes know that their next stop would be the buyer of the cotton and corn that would be planted as soon as they returned to the farm.

Jes was taken aback when Mr. Loving introduced him as "Mr." Jes. "He is my farm manager and knows more about farming than anyone in the county. We – he — wants to ask about the best seed to plant in some very fine soil. He has several different types of seed in mind."

Jes knew now why Mr. Loving had brought the largest wagon.

First, Jes inquired about the different types of most seeds that the buyer was aware of and used by most of the planters. He explained that there were several types and that the planter chose the variety best suited for his market. Jes fumbled around for a minute, then described the area of Mr. Loving's farm where he was most interested in planting.

"We's kinda late in gettin' da seeds in da groun' but with some long hours, we git it done." Jes turned toward his boss. "Mr. Lovin', I tink we need to be orderin' the seeds," he said. "We has almost 200 acres ta plants now, so I tinks we need ta do it."

Before they departed the seed merchant turned to Mr. Loving and asked, "Mister, just where did you find that nigger? He has more farming sense than all the folks around here, black or white. I sure would like to have him working for me."

"He is not a nigger," Mr. Loving said. "I object to that word, please don't use nigger. He's very sensitive about being a good person and that word is offensive to everyone except those here in the South."

The merchant cringed but said no more.

The long ride back to the farm was one of Mr. Loving asking Jes one question after another. Jes felt overwhelmed and gave his best answers. He was determined to stay close to this man regardless of all his crazy questions.

One thing Jes had been mulling over was the new barn.

"Boss, jus when does ya think you be havin' all da wood for da new tabacky curin' barn?" Jes asked after they'd returned to the farm. "If'n we get ta wood soon, durin' the firs' of the cold season, we's at leas' can put up most o'da big poles an maybe some of da outside walls. Tabacky won' be ready till late summer, so we's do mo' work after we's done da fields. I tink dat's important ta tink 'bout now."

"What big poles, Jes?"

Jes explained that the whole barn depended on a sturdy frame, since the walls had to be opened during the curing time. "If'n we doesn't has strong wall poles, it'll fall down wit da firs' strong wind. We counted da poles las' night but now I's do'n 'member. Dey has ta be strong if we dey goin' ta last and be big enough for da tobacco we grows. We be needin' at leas' four big poles foe each outside wall an four longer poles down da middle on each side." Jes was counting on his fingers as he spoke. "Now, if I be countin' right, dat's eight poles for da middle, da long sturdy ones, and eight mo' for da outside." Jes bent down and started to draw in the dirt. He made the shape of what he thought the barn would look like with the poles set in place. He then described where all the poles should be.

Mr. Loving nodded his head in understanding.

"Does we have any good hard woods for makin' such poles?

Scratching his soft beard, Mr. Loving had to think about what Jes had just shared with him. "Jes, I had to order most of the solid hard wood from up North and it took a number of months just to get it here. I will have to write a letter to the wood mill, I think it's in Illinois, and order what you have suggested. Just how long should the poles be, all of the poles? We need to have a measurement so that the mill won't send poles that don't work."

Jes had to admit that he needed to set out the size of the barn and then decide how much strength the long poles needed to have. "I's will get you da measurements early tomorrow morning, Boss."

Jes called the men that he wanted to start turning the soil and preparing it to be planted. It had been Jes's early decision to plant cotton where there had been tobacco planted but due to the sour soil, tobacco was to be planted near the stream to the far west of the farm, The soil there had been rotated from sugar beets to corn several times and was considered the best for a great crop of cotton. Jes laid out all the plans for the season of planting and selected the farm hands that would work each place. He knelt down so that he could draw and sketch just what he wanted to have the men do.

"Now, from here ta here. I's want ya three men ta make da furrows ready for da seed." He pointed to the chosen men. "You mens dat are lef', get da sack o'seed when dey git here an be ready ta start plantin' fas' as ya can. We needs ta have all da land done in a week. I knows ya can do it. I be ready ta help all I can." He saw the men hurrying to start.

Jes selected one of the more knowledgeable farm hands, Leroy, and they spent most of the morning measuring where the new barn was going to be. With nothing but a big ball of heavy twine, they walked back and forth, kicking dirt as they set out the outside of what Jes had decided the size of the barn should be. Stepping back some one hundred feet, he drove a heavy stick into the soft ground. Stepping off the distance from the stick to the closest side of where the new barn was to be, he informed his helper, "Dat mean da outside poles be at bes' eighty foot, an da center poles no shorter dan a hun'rud foot.

"I needs to get this information to da boss right's now." He turned, thanked Leroy for his help, then rushed back to the Boss's home. Jes learned a long time ago always to say thank you for anything and anyone that gave of himself for assistance in any matter.

After the new seed arrived, Jes stood by the sacks for a long time. Finally opening one of the sacks, he shoved his hand deep down into it. "Dis be da firs' seeds I has part in selectin'. Dey's my seeds. I's goin' ta make sure dat dey gets da bes' plantin' dat I's ever done." Looking up to the sky he again mumbled, "God, let me see what yous like ta do ta us po' color folk." Standing back straight, he felt just a little foolish at asking God to help him when he never had asked God for anything.

One thing that bothered Jes was a suitable place for all to have as a church. He had planned to speak to the boss about what might be done but he wanted to have a suggestion before asking. As he walked to the main house, he went over the only two places that he thought would do — the leather and harness building and one end of the barn. The barn seemed the best of his recommendations for the high rafters would allow better sound to be heard by all.

As he stepped to the side door, the youngest of the two colored ladies greeted him. "Come in, Mr. Jes. Da boss 'bout ta have me come fetch ya. He in da readin' room. Follow me."

Mr. Loving was sitting at a long table that was scattered with many different sheets of writing paper. "Come in Jes. I've been going over all my property to put on paper just what I would like to do about selecting the best for planting. Help me decide?"

"Boss, dat be fine but can I get dis off o'my chest firs'? I been askin' all da hans 'bout a place foe dem ta go ta church. I tinks da best place be at one end of da barn — da end dat faces west where da sun go down. Thataway, they be singing at da end of da day an' prayin' foe a better day come tomorra. Can we clean da mess an give dem a special place ta go ta church?"

Mr. Loving pushed back his chair and loudly proclaimed, "Only if you reserve a seat for me. I'm used to attending a church but not since coming to America. It would feel good to begin again. My England family was Catholic; do you have any idea what religious faith our hands feel bound to? Mr. Jes, you know what the hands need in order to be happy. If you need any material, let me know."

Jes wasn't amused when several of his friends began to tease him about his constant visits to the growing fields. "Jes, why do'n ya jus take some of dat corn to bed wif ya so ya can hear de stuff growin' and be ready for da early harvest."

Early Spring, 1845

With spring well on its way and only part of the planting in the ground, from early daylight to just after dark, the farm was in turmoil. Jes had selected the hands that seemed to do best with the mules and horses, putting them at plowing and furrowing the fields.

Leroy was the most entertaining hand of all. He would talk to the mules and ask them to do better as he worked the soil.

Jes, on this particular day, stopped Leroy and asked him, "Leroy, ya ask dat mule a lot of questions. Ain't his name Stubborn? He ever answer you back?"

It was a joke for Jes to ask but Leroy had an appropriate answer.

"Mr. Jes, I know's 'zackly what he say by da way he work. I's nebber has a mule be so smart in all m'days. Jus' watch. I's turn him 'round an start 'nother row."

Jes had carefully watched the words that Mr. Loving spoke and took the opportunity to remind Leroy that he should try to improve his use of words. "Like you just now said, 'nebber' when you should have said 'never.' Does that seem too difficult for you? Just try to do better, if you can. It will make it easier for you to talk to everyone. I sometimes say words like most of the colored do but I's trying to remember to say just like Mr. Loving."

Leroy just nodded his head and said that he would try and continued to work his magic with the mule. He didn't try to guide the mule with the harness straps but the mule made a perfect turn and started the new furrows. Looking at Jes, he smiled and seemed to say, "See how easy Matilda knows just what I wants her to do."

Some of the hands wondered if Jes had all his mental points for selection of some of the most important seeds. It would sound as if he was talking to them.

"Looky here little seed, I's goin' ta place ya in some vera fine soil, make sure dat ya get plenny o'fresh water an let ya begin ta grow ta a fine plant. Mr. Lovin' an I is sure in need o'the best cotton dat ya can make. Tries you bes' ta grow."

The other hands just shook their heads for they knew Jes had gone off his mind.

By the end of spring, every inch of Mr. Loving's farm was fully planted. Now, they could only wait for the new shoots of the crops to show their green side, then cultivating and weeding would take over.

Again, from first dawn to the last light, every field worker was hoeing the planted fields, removing the unwanted weeds and shaping up the furrows. It was a constant chore to cultivate almost all the crops and make sure that they were doing well.

By summer's end, the corn was ready for the harvest and cotton bolls were showing their first white inner stuff.

As the corn matured, the four field wagons were pulled by the most gentle of mules and as they were guided down the rows, the field hands pulled the ears of ready corn from the corn stalks, tossing them into the wagons. As each wagon was filled, it would be driven to Woodville and to the buyer.

It would take two weeks to harvest all the corn and the cotton would be next.

It was the custom for each hand, man or woman, to select a spot for their own garden where they planted some vegetables that they liked and that the farm did not plant. They would work in the farm fields all day, then just before the close of evening tend their private plot.

The new and bigger tobacco-curing barn had been finished, working piecemeal when there was no need for the hands to be working in the fields. On a cool afternoon when the day's work had been done, Mr. Loving called everyone to the equipment barn and stated that it was time to honor the completion of the best tobacco-aging barn in the county, if not the whole country.

"As a reward to everyone, I am adding another dollar to your pay. I want to thank each one for some very hard work." All the colored hands just smiled for they knew that they had done a good job.

Mr. Loving had five wagons for hauling any of the needed heavy items like the timbers for the new tobacco barn and above all, the crops to Woodville.

It was a long, all-day trip to deliver the harvested cotton and more so, the heavier corn. Jes needed and had selected and the hardest working hands, one as a wagon driver and the other as a helper.

The cotton gave the farm a problem. When it was harvested, the dry outer hull had sharp spines where the bolls broke apart. If the person doing the picking wasn't careful, the sharp point gave a very painful poke. The now loose puffs of cotton were dumped onto a wagon and sent to Woodville to be made into the large heavy bales. They averaged over five-hundred pounds each and were difficult to handle, often taking three men just to move each one, From Woodville they were shipped by rail to Chattanooga, Tennessee for further shipment to the mills.

Jes did not know if the coming end of harvest made him feel good, but as he watched most of the hands completing the last harvest of the cotton, he had a hankering to join them. During his days as just a slave farm hand, he had dragged the long cotton harvest sack along the rows of cotton. The sack was some twelve feet long and had two straps that went across his shoulders and allowed him to drag the sack without any other effort. If a good picker worked hard and knew what he was doing, he could sack some 400 pounds of harvested cotton. Not many could do that all day.

Jes had noticed that one of the ladies seemed to be better at picking cotton than any of the others, including the men. She was fast. Each opened bole was all but dried out and had very sharp points where the bolls came together. All of the pickers had sore fingers due to the boles sharp points.

At the end of the cotton season, Jes arranged with Mr. Loving to give her an extra dollar for her effort. It made her monthly income seven dollars.

It was the end of September, almost the end of the harvest season. It became a habit that for the evening dinner, many ears of the finest fresh corn was gathered and put into the big pot that was used to heat water.

Sometimes a pig would be slaughtered and cooked over an open fire made from seasoned hard oak wood.

Where and what kind of seasoning the cooks used was considered secret but almost everyone knew. It was herbs from the overgrown countryside, with some regular types to balance it off. Rubbed deep into the meat and left to dry, it was slow roasted over the fire.

The finished food was some of the tastiest ever served. Other times, Mr. Loving would select a prime steer, take a hindquarter, boning it and like the pork, then taking over 20 hours to slow bar-b-que the beef. This was always a special occasion for whatever reason the boss would think of.

With the end of the harvest season, Mr. Loving asked Jes to select the fattest steer and have it processed for a celebration at the end of harvest. Jes had already noted his choice of the critter that he wanted to have for the event.

With the harvesting complete, Mr. Loving asked Jes if he could visit him in his home. Jes had been invited to share several evening's meals with his boss so he was not concerned about the request. Jes felt that something special was going to happen so he put on the pair of almost new overalls and an old faded, but whole, shirt. He did not want the boss to think that he was always sloppy in his personal dress. One of the colored house ladies met him at the door and stated that Mr. Loving was in the study, waiting for him.

"He has a pile of papers laying out on the big table and is grinning like a cat, however a cat grins."

"Come on in Jes," Mr. Loving said. "I'm going over the sales of all the crops and find that we made a bigger profit than I had hoped for." He began to tell Jes how many wagon loads of corn and the many more of cotton that they had harvested. He did not mention the sugar beets, for they were not a high-demand product.

The tobacco was still curing in the barn. Jes had mentally tried to keep track of the wagon loads he had taken to Woodville and delivered to the buyer, with whom Mr. Loving had become friends. Jes was somewhat ashamed the he couldn't read and had voiced his wish that he could learn to just read the basic stuff.

There was so much that Jes now felt he didn't have and he wanted to learn as much as he could. He wasn't one to complain to the boss about any shortcomings.

Both men reviewed all the receipts and other general costs, including the monthly pay to all of the colored hands. Each different crop was discussed in full and when all was done, Mr. Loving turned to Jes.

"Mr. Jes, we have done very well for a first year and now it's important to see if we can do better next season. Do you have any good suggestions?"

Jes had reviewed the northern field that was set aside and planted only in hay but the soil seemed to be satisfactory for almost any kind of crop.

"All da sour smell be gone an the soil tase sweet. I tink we might should plant da two hun'rud acres in da corn or da cotton. Dat's where da money be, Mr. Lovin'."

The big surprise was sugar beets. Sugar had become short supplied and was earning high prices.

"I didn't know someone has made a automatic seeder. Does you remember buying one of dose contraptions? It works real fine."

Before Jes stood up, ready to leave, Mr. Loving asked Jes, "What do we need to do now besides put the fields to sleep for the winter?"

Rubbing his chin, Jes said that there was a great deal to do. "We can shalla disc da conefiel' an' plant a crop o'winter wheat dat make da hay. An all da farm equipmen' need service an set out o'da weather, ready foe nex' season. Mose' important is da animals. Da horses dey need shod, da shoes dey has now be worn down ta da hooves. Boss, da mules an 'specially da horses has ta have they hooves trim, an only Leroy do dat. We has a ton o'tings ta do. If ya don' mine, I's see ta all o'it."

Jes had a real passion for the care of all the animals. He sought out Leroy and inquired about his schedule of taking care of the mules and horses. In a closing comment Jes said,

"Be sure dat ya put new shoes on dat darn frien'ly mule. I tink he also need his feet trim."

For each of the next two years, the farm improved under the hard work of all the hands and the guidance of Jes.

Jes couldn't believe how fast two years had passed. Each year had been much better than the last with larger and larger profits to show for their hard work. Jes had switched some of the fields around so that the soil wasn't depleted of its good nutrients. He wasn't sure what an educated soils person would call it but he knew because at several of the past plantations one of those men would come and test the fields. He would always ask many questions and always remembered what he was told. Now he put that information to use and received great appreciation from Mr. Loving.

Midday, July 1846

It was a bright, sunny morning when it seemed that the whole colored community of the so-called hamlet of Spike came rushing to Mr. Loving's farm. Jes and most of Mr. Loving's hands knew that something bad had happened in the hamlet and they headed the mass off before they reached the main house. What struck Jes first were the tears rolling down almost everyone's dark cheeks. It took Jes much more time than he had thought to stop them and have them regain some of their composure.

Finally, one of the loudest ladies began to shout, "Dey's kilt him an jus hung him in da big oak tree. Dey's jus hung him foe no'ting an lef 'im hangin' in da tree. He be swingin' in da win' like a piece o'trash."

Jes was beside himself and he could not hear over the crying and shouting that all the hands were going through. Finally, one of the older men stepped out and said in a very pained voice, "Let Jes know what happen in da hamlet."

"Dis colored boy come into da white town an ask, "Where Mr. Lovin' has a ranch? I has a uncle dat work foe him an want ta find him. Afore he even say da nex' word, white hoo'lums, three of dem, put dey rope 'round his neck an be yellin' dat no nigger welcome in dis white people town. Den dey beat him wit big sticks on da head an' 'cross his poe skinny back. Af'er he weren't movin' no moe, dey strung him up in da tall oak tree jus as ya come into the place. He still hangin' high an swingin' in da win'."

Jes was staggered by what the man had said. Looking around he noted that some of the men had shot guns and the look of meanness, and a desire to kill on their faces.

In Jes's mind, he could see a slaughter about to happen and asked all the men with guns to put them down and take several deep breaths. "If'n you people, all of you's don't settle down, we's going to have blood flowing down dat dirt road and nothing will ever be da same. I needs ta has Mr. Lovin' listen to ya and give some goo' advice. So jus sit down a while, den we make some sense outta what happen."

Jes did not have to fetch Mr. Loving. He'd heard all the noise and walked to meet Jes, who was about half way to the main house. Jes stopped Mr. Loving and as best as he could, related what all the crying and shouting was about.

"Jes, you did the right thing. We need to calm everyone down and discuss what the colored people want to do now. Everyone needs to think about what an angry bunch of men and women on a rampage can do. We cannot let that happen. About how many of the colored are there?"

Jes didn't have time to count how many so he stated that there was a bunch, "Mayhap ever'one dat's in Spike plus dose dat live close.Maybe a half hun'rut or so."

The time of day that the mass marched to Mr. Loving's ranch was just before noon and now it was almost four o'clock. The tempers had cooled somewhat but there was still a lot of moaning and praying by the people.

Mr. Loving asked if everyone could be quiet. Then he asked, "Is that poor boy still hanging in the tree? That will never do. He must be brought down and have a proper burial with prayer and songs. So, if you have a preacher, or a man of God, let him arrange for the correct closing of this young man's life and give him the honor that he deserves. Is there a carpenter handy so that a good wooden coffin can be fashioned?"

It took less than an hour for everything to get organized. With Mr. Loving and Jes leading all of them, they marched into Spike.

There was not one person, white or colored, to be seen anywhere. The dirt street was completely empty and even the usual dogs weren't around.

At the eastern entry of Spike and the giant oak tree, everyone could see the still slightly swinging body of a black boy hanging from the largest limb of the tree. Some fifty feet before the tree, everyone stopped and just stared at the sick scene. Some of the colored people began again to moan and sing their most humbling song, "I Ain't Going To Tary here Any More."

Sweep it clean
Ain't going to tarry here

Sweep my house with the gospel room
Sweep it clean

Going to open my mouth to the lord
Ain't going to tarry here

O-o-o Lordy
Ain't going to tarry here

On to the rest of the song

Jes was the first to take hold of the boy's body while he directed several others to cut the rope and gently lay the body on a blanket.

Mr. Loving had seen a number of dead white people but never one of color. He was caught up in that there was no change in the color of the boy's skin and features. It caused his bile to rise and it was all he could do to keep from vomiting. It made him lose his stature and Jes quickly caught his arm to steady him and keep him from falling.

Four of the men gently picked up the body and asked several of the women, "Just where does you lady folks want us'n to lay this poor soul so that he can be made ready to meet his Lord? Two of the older ladies both said at the same time, "To our house, and just lay him's on da' bed. We's will do the rest."

None of the people wanted to leave. Many of them wanted to hunt down the three white men that had done such a ruthless crime caught and treated in the same way.

Jes shouted, "Don' be goin' off da deep en' an becomin' jus' like da whites. Dey'll get they comeuppance an I's sure de Lord know jus' who do dis an have already plan foe they punishment. We go get dat po' boy body in da kine earth. Den mayhap we agree 'bout what ta do. Dey's no law here, mayhap we gets da law from Woodville ta pass da judgment. Dey's s'pose ta have a hones' sheriff."

On the following day at noon, some two hundred, mostly people of color, met at the colored cemetery and began a ceremony unlike any that

Mr. Loving had ever seen or heard, singing wonderful spiritual songs, moaning, crying and outright screaming.

It was decided that the grave was to be at the most significant part of the colored cemetery. The entire cemetery was just two acres in size and was in complete disarray Weeds were everywhere and the few head stones were at a slant or turned over due to poor settings. The final spot was on a slight rise near the back of the cemetery that had a strong tree giving some shade to the site.

Jes made a mental note to clean up the coloreds' resting place and make some new markers where the names were known.

First, a small group of the colored began to sing,

Nobody knows de trouble I've seen
Nobody knows de trouble but Jesus
Nobody knows de trouble I've seen
Glory Hallelujah!

Sometimes I'm up, sometimes I'm down
Oh, yes Lord
Sometimes I'm almost to de groun
Oh, Yes, Lord

If you get there before I do
Oh, Yes, lord
Tell all-a my friends I'm coming too
Oh, yes, Lord

A great baritone voice sang "Swing Low, Sweet Chariot" and then the last song "Steal Away to Jesus."

There was an ongoing soft, almost a hum, of low voices praying all during the singing.

Mr. Loving stood with a steady stream of humble tears sliding down his face. He had never seen a body so beat up and hanging from a tree that was the main symbol of the hamlet. Jes, stooped shouldered like he had the whole world on his shoulders, joined him.

Jes had never been one of great religious faith but he had to admit, this service asked him deeply about his bond to his God. With the tears also sliding down his much wrinkled face, he said, "I guess I has ta do someting 'bout dat."

All the way, the mass of colored people very quietly walked to the plantation of the owner who had attended the service and he had agreed to serve the usual after-burial feast. There was a lot of talking among the colored people and the few white attendees. Jes stood far off to one side and observed. At this painful time, they seemed to just be normal and not at each other's throats. He mumbled to himself, "Lord, why can't it be like this all the time, peace in our valley."

Two weeks went by with no further problems regarding the hanging of the colored boy.

Jes was having his second cup of precious coffee as he always did, sitting on the front steps of his new home. At first, he thought he was seeing things. In the early light, a figure was slowly walked up Mr. Loving's road. The first thought that crossed Jes's mind was, Here's another poor colored man wanting to come to work for Mr. Loving.

As he became close, Jes could see that there was a deep troubled frown on his rugged face. *Now what?*

"Mr. Jes, dey's doodit," the man said. "'Bout all da colored in de neighborhood cactched dem white boys dat hung da colored boy. Den dey went an done ta dem whats dey did ta da boy. Dat weren't 'nuf so dey burn da biddins. Now dey no mo' houses in da place. All da whites done lef'. Ain't even no dogs lef'. I's afrait dat some real bad killins gonna happen. Mayhap yous an yo' boss come settle things a bit?"

The only time that Jes had felt so frightened was when he was just a kid on the boat that had brought him to this crazy land. As he hurried to Mr. Loving's home, crazy thoughts were screaming through his mind. He imagined a war of the white people and the colored people all laying dead in the dirt road, with him the only one left standing. Cold shudders went all the way down to his behind as he approached the main house. Mr. Loving had seen Jes hurrying and met him on the front porch.

"Jes, what has you in such a boil this early in a new day?"

Jes repeated all the information that the man had told him and watched as Mr. Loving's facial expression went from very pleased to the same fear that Jes was showing.

"Jes! We have to get to the people as soon as we can and try to stop any further killings between the whites and the colored. This is going to demand some kind of law to put a stop to this craziness. Maybe you should hitch up the carriage with the two fastest horses and be ready to rush to Woodville."

As they traveled through Spike, the three bodies of the men were hanging from the same large tree limb that the colored boy had been hanging from.

In Spike, they found some one hundred colored people milling around with shotguns and pistols, ready to fight anyone that stood in their way. The hamlet was just as the messenger had stated, only smoldering coals were left

Both Jes and Mr. Loving loudly began to yell.

"This is no way to settle anything and all that you will do is bring many of the area white folks charging to wipe out all the colored peoples. They seem to want to do away with all of you anyway. Don't give them an excuse. Jes and I will rush to Woodville and ask the law to come and settle everything. Will all of you give us that much time before you go completely crazy?"

Neither Jes nor Mr. Loving could understand why the sheriff wasn't in town. They learned that someone had warned the sheriff that Jes and Mr. Loving were coming to Woodville and he suddenly had to go fishing. Mr. Loving inquired about an Army Post and was directed to a small one just at the edge of the town.

Again, they were treated as if they had a bad disease. The Captain that was in charge listened for the explanation, then informed the two men that Spike was out of his authority and he couldn't do anything about their concern. Mr. Loving asked where the head Army authority might be located and was told that it was several days away and that a letter was the only thing that could be sent.

Mr. Loving shook his head. "Don't you crazy people understand that a white and colored war is about to occur and you don't give a damn about it?"

He and Jes walked back to their carriage and started home. Neither said a word until they were almost to the ranch. Jes mumbled something about how crazy the people were in this country and that he wished that he was back in his Africa.

As the two rode into what used to be Spike, Many of the colored had gone back to their plantation or home but soon they were surprised to learn that about half had gone to Mr. Loving's ranch with most of the ranch's colored. An older colored gentleman told them that one of Mr. Loving's hands had scolded everyone about the burning of Spike and shamed them into returning to their own places. Instead, many of them wanted to be close to the man and went to Mr. Loving's place.

Mr. Loving was now in a quandary. "Why my place, and just what am I going to do with some 40 to 50 people to look after?" He just shook his head and looked at Jes for some kind of answer.

Jes simply said, "Da good Lord will provide." Jes had no idea where the words came from and how he had never thought much about asking the Lord for anything.

Everything became quiet when a white sheriff appeared. "I'm a federal marshal and here to look into the killer of three white youths. Who is in charge of this place?"

Mr. Loving introduced himself as the spokesperson for all the people in the area, black or white, knowing that there were no white people other than himself for miles.

The moment Mr. Loving spoke, the sheriff became very hostile and demanded to have all the colored gathered in one place so that he could keep an eye on them. Again, Mr. Loving spoke much louder.

"Sheriff, or whatever you call yourself. You have no rights or law in this place. Just where were you when the white people here hanged a poor colored boy because he asked directions to my ranch? Just where were you? And now you come rushing in here demanding that all the colored be herded into one place so that you can charge them with some kind of crime. Just what kind of law are you?"

The sheriff made like he was going to reach for a pistol when one of the colored, unnoticed by any one, pointed a double barreled shot gun and plainly stated, "Mister, don't even tink 'bout bein' foolish. I can clear ya outa ya saddle afore ya can say anythin'."

The sheriff stopped in the middle of his movement and whirled his horse and men about, yelling that he would be back.

Back at the ranch, Jes noted that all of Mr. Loving's hired hands and the mass of colored folks from who knew where were all in the back where the main cooking area was. To both men's amazement, some of the hands had taken most of the cured pork from the smoke house and were preparing a meal for everyone.

Mr. Loving sat staring. "Jes, can you beat that? I guess the way I treat my people has rubbed off, and now they think about taking care where care is needed. Let's join them and have something to eat before it's all gone. My people sure make me proud."

As they sat and ate, the older of Mr. Loving's hands came over and said, "I hopes dat ya'll not put out 'cause I's brought dem folks ta ya ranch. I not be knowin' what ta do ta break up da angry talk afore it r be out of han'. I jus' had ta do somthin'." Then he repeated his concern that Mr. Loving might be angry.

Jes stepped up, put his arm around the man, and assured him that Mr. Loving was more than pleased and he had been right to have a lot of them come to the ranch. The eating and much better attitude of everyone was something to see. All the colored folks were hugging everyone, coming over to Mr. Loving, and telling him how pleased that he was part of the people, the good earth, and their friend. "You's da onliest white man to be good to us colored folks."

Jes and Mr. Loving began the new spring planting season with three changes in crop rotation. Jes paid special attention to the soil quality and added amendments when the soil showed a decline of the right minerals. The tobacco showed the most profit over the first two years so Jes decided to add fifty more acres of the best variety. New corn, Jes had kept the best of the last years' corn crop for seed to be planted the coming year. The corn was the finest that had been grown on the ranch and promised to be even better when used as seed.

He pushed his hand deep down into that sack of seed to feel the strength of the coming season. The corn would be planted last because the hot summers, with little rain, allowed the fall crop to take advantage of late rains and cooler weather. As the hands finished the corn and all stood around and enjoyed the final effort, Jes calmly said. "O.K peoples, now its time to celebrate. Tonight we will Bar-B-Cue the fatted calf, well steer, and just be pleased that all we have to do is watch the seed grow."

Mr. Loving and Jes had been making their monthly visit to Woodville for needed supplies and always enjoyed spending time with the seed merchant and the buyer of almost everything that Mr. Loving grew. The buyer praised them for the outstanding crop. It was a good time to learn of new types of seeds and other news.

On this particular visit, both men noticed a different attitude among many of the local residents. As they sat in the buyers' cubbyhole of an office, Mr. Loving asked the buyer, "Just what is wrong with the town? Everyone seems to be on a sharp edge."

The buyer informed them that the new president was going to make a law that would free all the slaves and it had caused many in the South to start talking about leaving the Union and forming their own country.

"So far, it's been nothing but talk but if the South does secede from the Union, it will mean one hell of a war. Can you imagine, brother against brother, father against sons and on down the line? It will mean the total ruin of our country. I suggest that you make plans to plant every acre in the best cotton next year. If the wheels come off our country, cotton will be the biggest moneymaker of any other crops. I wouldn't plan on any sugar beets or even corn. Corn will be important, but as I said, cotton will be in the greatest demand."

Jes looked at Mr. Loving and had a deep frown. "I guess we had better start making plans to do as he suggested."

It was the first time that Mr. Loving noted that Jes had spoken his words without the usual colored slang. "Jes, have you been studying how I speak?"

"I's… I been studying how you use words and tryin' to remember. Yes boss, I thought I better take in some education and learn to try and keep up with you and all the other white folks. I tried to impress the hands to pay 'tention and try to improve their speaking. Some's done pretty good but others just think it's a waste of time. Dey wants to stay colored and speak da same's way. I gather them together each night that wants to learn and we talk 'bout how to speak like the white folks do. Be nice to have a regular class, get more folks to learn."

Mr. Loving took careful note of Jes's comments.

None of the farm hands on Mr. Loving's ranch showed any concern about the news that sometime in the future, they might be free people. One commented, "I's as free as I's eber going ta be. If'n crazy folk has ta kill each uder, jus' wha' kine freedom dat be?"

There was an increase of the colored slaves trying to escape to the North and the flow through the ranch became a flood. With each new person heading North, either Jes or Rube would usher them to the shelters deep in the woods of Mr. Loving's ranch, giving them some food and a warning about white slave hunters going from one plantation to another, looking for runaway slaves. It was a brutal capture when a slave was found. He or she would be beaten until they were unconscious and sometimes killed. None of the slaveholders seemed to care if they lost a slave to this kind of brutality. The escaping slave would be gone the following morning.

For almost a year, there was nothing but false information floating around their small part of Georgia. Occasionally a group of what seemed like self-appointed bands of men would come parading along the dirt road and yelling, "You will soon be in the rebel army." The farm hands just watched and glared at the men as they passed by.

The crops for the year were as expected — the most bountiful of any so far. Jes had attempted to increase the cotton acreage but the seed had barely sprouted when the late summer rains washed them out of the soil and they dried in the following sun. He began to try to understand how best to plant for the next season. Mr. Loving had left all the decisions of farming up to Jes and he took the responsibility very seriously. Evenings could find him gazing out across all the farmland and mumbling to himself how he should plant that here and that there. When the seasons started, he would know exactly where each seed was to go and in what part of the land.

Fall was the harvesting part of each year and the present harvest was at hand. The chosen hands that did the hauling last year were the same ones for the coming season. Jes had them grease all the wheel hubs, check the fasteners to the horses, and soap the harnesses with special grease so that they were in the best shape.

Corn was the first to be ready and wagon after wagon could be seen slowly moving through the cornfields as the hands pulled the ears from the stalks and tossed them into the wagon. Jes got a great deal of emotional pride as the wagons filled with the golden corn for he knew that they would bring the best dollar for the boss and pride to everyone on the farm. Again, Jes saved the best corn kernels for the next year's seed. This had become a standard practice each season. There was no cotton to be harvested so the hands had some time for their own.

The oncoming winter was deemed one of the worst in the south in many years. Jes had most of the fields put to bed before the freezing rain and sleet covered the land. He would meet with Mr. Loving for several hours bemoaning the lousy weather but assure the boss that come spring, they would be more than ready.

Winter, 1859

It was a cold miserable day when Mr. Loving asked Jes to come to his house. Mr. Loving was sitting in the space that he used as an office and had a large fire burning in the giant fireplace.

"Jes, sit down. I've been thinking about your wants and the wants of all the other hands, to have some good education for mostly speaking and in its turn, reading, writing. I have written several friends in the North asking them if they know of a colored, well-educated teacher that might want to move to the South and be the teacher for some 47 very fine people of color. I was about to give up hope, then the last time we visited Woodville I received two letters from two different people asking about a teaching position here in the South. He handed Jes the two letters, and he immediately reminded Mr. Loving that he could not read.

"Oh, I forgot. Maybe if one of these people really come, we can take care of that."

Jes asked Mr. Loving, "Jus' wha' does you has in mine, boss? One of dem come now while we's not doin' much work, we has all winter ta learns. We's has ta make some room foe da teacher ta works in but dat's no problem. Y'al knows jus' who deese people be?"

"No, but one is a woman and she seems the best qualified by her education. If you approve, I want to invite her to come for a visit and make her own decision. She can have one of the extra rooms in my house if she wants and all of you can meet her for your own impression."

Jes had no way of making such an important decision and told him so. "She come, it be a great time fore eberyone. When ya tink she be answerin'?

Mr. Loving let Jes know that he felt that it was important enough that he was going to write her a letter that night and have one of the hands take it to Woodville early the next day. I would guess the way mail is going, it will be a month before we can expect some kind of response. That's the best we can do, Jes."

He asked Jes to sit down and rest his bones while he wrote the letter.

Mr. Loving wrote that his farm hands wanted to learn how to speak like the white man and that there were some forty fine colored hands that worked for him. He added that they were all very good people and deserve to have what is best for them. He signed, Mr. Loving, Loving's Ranch.

As Jes got up to leave, he turned to Mr. Loving and asked, "Mr. Lovin', jus where you learn all dem words?"

For over three months, there was no response from either person that Mr. Loving had hoped to bring to the ranch to teach all the hands a better way of using the English language. A rider traveled to Woodville each week just to pick up any mail that might have arrived.

It was on a beautiful but very cold winter afternoon of 1860 when a smartly dressed colored lady was noted arriving at the farm. She was riding in an open sort of carriage with one horse to power it.

"Do you have either a Mr. Loving or a Mr. Jes on this beautiful plantation?" she asked.

"Firs off," replied the ranch lady, "dis not a plantation, it's be a darn good ranch an yes, we do has da people's you axe 'bout. I's can gets dem foe ya or y'all can drives ta da main house an axe foe Mr. Lovin'. He be da one dat own da ranch an Jes da main man an boss of da farmin'." She then pointed to the main house.

At first, the young lady looked somewhat startled at the way the ranch lady spoke. Then, before she said anything, she remembered just why she found herself in this different place, a farm and not a plantation.

Mr. Loving met the lady at his front door and invited her to please step down. "It's hot and I am sure that you want a nice cold drink."

She quickly introduced herself as the receiver of a letter that inquired about a special position as a teacher of some special people of color. "I am

Nan Holton from Chicago. You know where Chicago is, don't you?" She smiled one of the brightest smiles that Mr. Loving had ever seen.

"Dear lady please join me in the shade, it's far too uncomfortable here in the sun and my house maid will bring us some fresh cold drinks. What would you like to drink?" Mr. Loving asked another house person to fetch Jes. "He's my manager of almost everything that goes on at this farm and is the one that asked for help in learning to speak properly. He has been with me over nine years and some of the other hands, now for almost ten years. I don't do anything around here without first asking Jes."

Jes was quickly ushered into the sitting room with what he thought was a most attractive young colored lady.

Before Mr. Loving could introduce Jes, Nan stood up and quickly said, "I guess that you are responsible for my coming here." The lady then reached down into her over large bag and withdrew the letter Mr. loving had sent seeking a teacher. "I hope that we can come to an agreement for the teaching position. I already think this farm is a wonderful place to be."

Jes could not speak. First, Nan was the most attractive lady of any color that he had ever seen. Second, she just looked smart and very professional. He didn't mumble this time, he held out his hand and softly stated, "Mose pleased ta meet ya an am lookin' forewad ta goin' ta yous school." Jes then sat down feeling very foolish.

Mr. Loving took over the remaining brief meeting by asking Nan if she was serious about becoming the teacher for his farm hands.

Nan responded by asking, "Why is your plantation, beg pardon — ranch — different than any of the others? All I have read about and the few that I have seen, are all adamant to be called plantation. Is there a reason?"

Jes beat Mr. Loving to the explanation. "Miz Horton, Mr. Lovin' not be from 'merica. He from a far away place call Englan' an they do thins dif'rent. He threaten anyone who call us 'slave' or 'nigger.' He don' let dat be. An he pay each hand fore they work. No udder place do such a respec'ful thin fore they peoples." Jes could see by the look on the lady's face that this came as a great surprise.

Before any more words could be said, Mr. Loving asked the two housekeepers to bring some cold refreshments and maybe some of that fresh cake that you have been fussing over. "Yes-sah, Mr. Lovin'."

Mr. Loving went on to explain the house arrangements for Miss Holton. She had no objection of a private room and sharing the dining with the two housemaids and Mr. Loving.

The housemaid that always took over gently took Miss Horton up the stairs to a special bedroom that had a massive window that overlooked the farm. It had been the original owner's bedroom and had been reserved for a potential guest. Miss Horton must have made up her mind before she started her journey to the South for she had two large suitcases and an over-stuffed carrier.

Miss Horton gave Mr. Loving a list of writing material for him to get the next time he visited Woodville. He was so pleased with what was going to be the beginning of teaching his field hands that he sent one of them to Woodville on a special trip. The hand was to go to Mr. Loving's friend who bought all his farm products and ask him to help. Mr. Loving was surprised when the man returned much faster than expected. The friend had taken the farm hand personally and made sure of the needed materials. To top it off, Mr. Loving's friend sent a double order and wrote in a note, "The extras are on me."

The area that was used for church services was also turned into a schoolroom. Tables and benches replaced the usual benches used for church and the tables were about half as wide as a regular table. When the farm hands first viewed them, there was a hand clapping session and a lot of, "Thank you, Lords."

The following day, Jes had made sure that at the close of the regular working day, every one of the colored hands were sitting quietly at a table with hands clasped in front and smiles that would make anyone excited.

Mr. Loving and Jes traveled to Woodville on one of their regular supply trips. The town was in an uproar. Troops in gray were everywhere and the flag of the South was the only one flying from many doors and flag posts.

Mr. Loving sought out his friend that bought all his crops and asked, "Just what in hell has happened?"

"Richard, my friend, the new president, Mr. Lincoln, has declared that all people of color are not to be held as slaves. He's threatening something called the Emancipation Proclamation. I don't know just what that means but it is sure to mean trouble for all slave owners. The vote to abolish slavery is being considered now and the South has declared that if it passes, the South will secede from the Union. Everyone knows that war with the North is just a few weeks away. It is a very sad time for everyone. May God help us.

"Dear friend, It will mean much of the things you grow will be in greater demand, so maybe you and your field boss might want to think about what you want to plant. Cotton will be the most in demand product. We can be of some help but seed will be in short supply."

Mr. Loving walked back to where Jes was putting some of the supplies in the wagon.

"Jes, I have some troubling news. I know that you've noticed the men in the gray uniforms parading around bragging and acting belligerent, waving mean looking guns. I just learned that a war between the states is just around the corner. Mr. Lincoln has declared that slavery will be abolished and that all slaves are to be set free. I do not know how this will make you and all the other hands on the farm feel, but it will mean disaster for everyone that any war brings with it. Believe me Jes, I don't understand killing each other over such a cruel issue."

Jes bowed his head as if in prayer. "Mr. Lovin', I tink dat what'er Mr. Lincoln do be da bes' for da whole country. I knows not all da colored folk at da farm will change they minds. We be mostly happy and don't know any better place ta go. Mr. Lovin', you stuck with us, like it or not. If war comes, it be terrible."

For the first time, Mr. Loving had noticed that Jes's speech was very much improved and commented, "Jes, you're starting to use the words more like Miss Horton teaches and they have a great effect on you. You're easier to understand."

On the return trip to the farm, they discussed the statement the seed supplier made about the demand for much more of the farmer's yield, especially cotton. "Why cotton?" asked Jes. As far as he knew, they just make clothing and such from it. "Why they need so much?"

"Mr. Jes, the whole world uses a great deal of high quality cotton for many things and much of our cotton is sold to other countries. That's where they say the South will be able to trade for weapons, ammunitions and food items. If we plant more cotton than last year, sad as it sounds, we can make a great deal more money. As you know, our cotton, corn and even the sugar beets brought more per ton than any of the other farms, well plantations. You don't know how much I owe you for rebuilding all the fields and making a wonderful bunch of hard working folks out of all the colored's hands. I know that they seem very happy in their work and homes. Isn't that right?"

Jes just nodded and smiled as the horses continued on their way. He felt that he had put his heart and soul into every hand full of soil of Mr. Loving's ranch

Nearing the ranch, Jes spoke up. "Boss, you want to plant more cotton? In which fields? We have ta start plannin' now if we going ta be ready in time. It gonna take more hard work but I knows all da hands be more than pleased ta do what'er it takes." Jes was making great effort to put Miss Horton's teachings to use and was making progress.

"One other ting, Boss. I notice how you be sayin' words an I be wantin' ta git some better learnin'. I tink most of da others want to become better talking like you. Now dat Miss Horton be here, you tink she want ta teach all us colored folk better speaking?"

Mr. Loving gave Jes an approving glance. "Mr. Jes, I have been thinking much about the same thing; that is about helping any of the ranch hands to become clearly better speaking. Not in the typical clipped words that almost all people of color use. I will be more than glad to help. Now about the planting, that will be up to you. You know better than I what fields have the best and proper soil for which crops. Just tell me and I will get the seed. You are right about planning now.

"Jes, what am I paying each worker each month? The big profit will allow me to maybe add a dollar or two to each hand's pay. Don't say anything about that to the others but I need to show how much I appreciate their hard work."

"Boss, what you tink—? Darn, there I go again. I need to pay more attention to the teacher's instructions. What will happen ta da colored folks if Mr. Lincoln sets 'em free? Not many have a place ta go and they'll not want ta stay with a slave owner. I knows dat words have already passed around 'bout you payin' all da hands and threatening anyone dat calls dem 'slaves' or 'niggers.' Them's mean words, Mr. Lovin'."

Jes reminded Mr. Loving that several slaves who felt they were already a freed people had walked to Mr. Loving's ranch to ask for work. Jes had talked to all of them, reminded each that the final decision had not been made and that their slave owners still considered them property and had sent their field bosses to retrieve the runaways.

"I told them, if you don' go back ta da plantation you come from, da bad man get meaner. Y'all must wait until things change, den you can goes where'er yous want."

Jes had begun to plan for the next year's planting season. He could not write so he drew stick pictures of the different crops and even how much seed that he thought each different crop would take. He wanted to impress Mr. Loving that he could think and make solid plans for the future. It took three evenings to finish his project. On the fourth evening, Mr. Loving had invited Jes to share dinner with him again. At least once a week this happened and Jes looked forward to the exchange of information and the great evening meal.

"Now Jes, what was it that you wanted to go over with me?"

Jes unfolded the several sheets of his drawings and apologized for his lack of being able to read, then added, "If that teacher starts teaching all of us better English speaking an writin', I'm sure I can do much better." He then began to explain the sheets of paper he had unfolded. "Boss, this what I been thinkin' 'bout next year's plantin'."

Jes went through each planting acreage and explained each crop with stick drawings as well as what would be needed come planting time. Mr. Loving took extra time reading each page and when he was finished, commended Jes on a very fine job and asked just how he could help.

"Boss, all's I needs is for ya ta get da seed in time for us ta go ta work. All the fields be turned an the furrows be where they needed. Dey be fine and ready. Boss, they's some ode plows needs replacing. We done fixed 'em far more dan dey be able to be fixed."

As Jes and Mr. Loving discussed the ranch's problems, Jes was watching Nan's reaction to the way he was speaking. She frowned when Jes spoke the usual colored way. He thought, *She going ta be stiff with her lessons.*

Troubling Days

Jes was not one to take hard drink and when Mr. Loving offered him a drink to celebrate everyone's best year, he declined by saying that all his life he couldn't understand why grown men had to have such bad tasting stuff to say thanks for a good job. Or worse, get stumbling down drunk because they failed in some way.

By letter, Nan received word from a friend in the North that the president's words on the Emancipation Proclamation had become final on January 1, 1863, and that letter was dated some months ago. The letter also said that hundreds of colored folks were streaming North and so many had escaped the South that a camp had been set up with a school so the young ones could get some real learning.

Mr. Loving and Jes wondered if Miss Horton would go back to Chicago to teach at that school. They said that they would ask and then beg her to stay at the Loving ranch.

Spring was just around the next bend. The farm had been in a sweat for several weeks. Warm weather made sweating very easy when hard work was in progress. All the fields had been plowed and some made ready for seed. Mr. Loving and Jes had traveled to Woodville and acquired most of the seed that would be planted early. Mr. Loving had bought a new double plow and the first automatic both cotton and corn seeders seen in the area. The new seeders would make planting much easier and faster, saving about half of the usual hand planting of each crop. It worked fine on the cotton and corn but would not help with the tobacco. The sugar beets, and tobacco were small new plants had to be placed one by one in the rows that were prepared different than the others.

It was after the evening meal and all the farm hands gathered in the new schoolroom. Miss Horton stood in the front of the group. There was a new crazy looking board nailed across the back of the room. Across the board, in very good handwriting were the letters NAN HORTON. Everyone knew that the teacher was Miss Horton and was somewhat puzzled by the writing.

She began, "I want to teach everyone the best way to say general words that many of the white people use. It's not hard but you have to want to learn. If all of you who want to learn just concentrate on each lesson until you have it in you mind, that will get the learning done. Now let's get to work."

Jes sat in the very back row and everyone knew that he was going to see that no one acted foolish about the words that Miss Horton was trying to teach. Slowly, Jes stood up and made one of the seldom speeches that he would ever make.

"The lady in front of the room will be helping all of us to be better at the white man's way of talking. It will help all of us to be sure of ourselves and give us more confidence in dealing with the white folks. This ain't something to learn lightly and anyone who wishes to not learn, well, they can leave now."

Miss Horton began to speak to her students, "People, I will learn each of your names as soon as I can. In the meantime, let me tell you a little about me.

"I graduated from a Chicago University five years ago. I earned a degree in education because I wanted to try to help the many people of color in that part of our country. I was humbled and honored when your Mr. Loving asked me to come to this wonderful ranch and meet all of you. Don't be afraid to ask questions, for they are a big part of learning. If anyone does not understand a statement and wants to have it repeated, just raise your hand so I know you want ask a question and I will answer it at that time."

No one raised a hand, so she went on to let all the people know what was going to happen in her class.

For several months, at the close of the day when all work was done, everyone met in the classroom and listened to Nan discuss one word at a time, then ask each person to repeat it until she was sure that the old way was removed from their speech. Some tried to learn, a few simply had no interest or motivation to sit in a room where they were being told something that they did not understand.

Jes was disturbed when several of the colored began to stay home instead of attending Miss Horton's class. He cornered the men and they said that they found no real need to learn how the white men spoke. The two months showed a small amount of progress for the farm hands had a problem separating the old from the new way of saying a word they had used wrongly for many years.

Finally, Jes asked each one of the hands if they would select a partner and go over one word at a time until it was branded in their minds. In just two weeks, Jes and Nan noted a big difference not only in speaking the words but in their attitudes. Jes felt that he and Nan had won.

Jes was determined to learn so he asked Miss Horton, Nan, to please spend some extra time in private with him.

April 12, 1861 — Civil War

Without any warning, several of the southern states declared their state to be a separate and sovereign state and had no intention of doing away with slavery. A civil war was days and not more than a month away. Jes asked Mr. Loving just what it would mean to all the hands. Mr. Loving was not too sure but he assured them that he would do his utmost to protect them.

"We'll go on trying to plant the crops as we have done all these years and expect to be treated fairly and with due respect. Mostly, it will depend on our being able to obtain the best seed .It is a very sad day when a country is divided in such a way where a war seems to be the only answer.

"It's the big money and large landholders with many slaves that are causing this to happen. I never thought that I would see such a war happen, and if I had, I would not have invested here.

"Remember Jes, our ranch is somewhat out of the traffic and may not be bothered very much. Regardless, all of us will have to plan for some military activity to pass through here. I have no idea what we can do. Mostly, they will want to take all our crops, cattle and other foodstuff. There will be nothing that we can do to stop them and I do not want any of my people to get hurt. Do you understand what I mean? If any of them demand anything, just give it to them and do not cause any trouble."

The hands seemed satisfied with the response of Mr. Loving and slowly walked back to their work talking about what they had just heard and voicing their opinions.

It was just three weeks when word was received about the New Southern States. Almost all of the Southern states had declared sovereignty and started to train their armies. As expected, more men on horseback came riding through the farm asking war type questions.

Fort Sumter had been fired on and all hell was breaking loose. Jes had no idea what or where the fort was located, but all the town of Huntsville was in an uproar over the event and was underway. Jes again solemnly bowed his graying head and whispered a pleading prayer for the craziness to stop.

A state of utter confusion existed on the farm. Meager news about the status of the Negro people on plantations was so sketchy that none of them knew what was going to happen to them. Some on the plantations were sure that they would be lined up and shot and others were sure that every tree would have a slave hanging from the limbs.

Jes was in a complete state of fear. He knew that Mr. Loving would not allow any harm done to his people but if an army came marching thru, what could he do? With his head bent down to his chest, he slowly walked to Mr. Loving's home, trying to make up questions that he wanted an answer to so that he could settle down the farm hands.

Mr. Loving had been waiting for Jes to arrive. He knew that Jes would be very concerned about what was to happen to all of them and he didn't have an answer.

In England many years ago, there had been invaders and wars to try to protect most of the people but the big wars were for the land that was held by rich landowners. Many of the people wouldn't support the English people because of the way the landowners treated them. Much like what was happening in the South now. Mr. Loving felt the whole weight of the world on his shoulders and didn't like it.

"Come in Jes, I know what's on your mind, the farm hands and all this war. No one knows what is going to happen but most Southerners are promising a war. If that happens, I'm going to try to keep our farm out of everything. I know that the southern army will come, taking everything that they want, mostly food items and livestock. I think maybe we should move all the cattle to the far north field into the woods where there are a lot of trees to give them shelter. The hay is still uncut and should be all the food that they need. As to the pigs, I have no idea where we could put them. Just the odor will give them away. Maybe we should slaughter a many as we can and keep that smoke house full. We can hide smoked pork and maybe chickens.

"The only thing that I can think of now about the colored hands is to just keep out of sight as much as they can and go about the farm's work as always. We just have to keep up with all that will be going on and do the best we can. Do you have any other suggestions, Jes?"

"Boss, I've not thought so much about the animals as you recommended, I'll have the men start taking care of them now. I'm mostly concerned about the ladies. I heard that the crazy troops often rape and beat up on them for no reason. I'm going to keep my old shotgun loaded and handy just in case. Let just one of those bastards set a hand on any one of them and my gun will take revenge.

"I'm also very concerned about Nan, She's not used to the way coloreds are treated in the South and may not like to stay out of sight. I have taken a special liking to that lady and will not let anything happen to her.

"Mr. Loving, if you have no other thing to talk about, I had best get going and have the men do what is needed."

Mr. Loving cut in with Jes's statement about Nan Horton. "So fancy the lady, do you, Jes? That's wonderful. She is a very nice person. Does she know how you feel? At this time, it might be very important to let her know and have some kind of understanding." Even with the hard times ahead, Mr. Loving had a smile on his aging face.

"No, Boss, I have no thinking about a wife. I seen many older people bear children into this crazy world and I don't want to add to it. A wife might be very nice, but children are always the next thing to happen." Jes hurried out to get the men to do as Mr. Loving suggested.

Most of the hands must have sensed what Jes and Mr. Loving were going to discuss. They were standing at the barn with sad looks on their faces. The one that liked to be called Bones stepped out and in his almost correct speaking way, asked, "Mr. Jes, can you's tell us what is going to happen with all the war coming down on our difficult lives?"

Jes stepped forward to be right in the face of all of the men.

"Friends, I am not a mister, I am just plain Jes." With a little anger in his voice, he said loudly, "No one will call me Mr. from now on, do all of you understand?

"Now, Mr. Loving made several very good suggestions and we had better get with the first one." He called out the men by their names and directed them to take all of the cattle except the milking ones, and put them in the far pasture where they could graze and have plenty of water from the stream. They'd have plenty of fine grass and be almost hidden from the Southern troops that will want to just take them for food.

"Now for you other men, I have the most lousy job of all. We have to clean out the smoke house and put in some bigger shelves. We're going to slaughter almost all the pigs that are ready and hard smoke the meat. We can't hide the pigs but the smoked meat, well we have many places to hide the meat and keep it from spoiling. If we do it the hard smoke way, the meat will last much longer and it only takes three more days to do the smoking. We also need to gather a pile of the best hard woods like wild apple and hickory to do the smoking. You'll be on you own, so get to it."

It was a real scramble as the men broke up into groups and began. Some headed for the smoke house and the others for the trees at the back of the big pasture. There were many squealing pigs making their last effort to stay alive, as they were made ready for the smoke house. Slaughtered pigs hung from almost every tree branch that could hold the weight of the slaughtered animal.

Jes was totally surprised when two men asked, "Mr. Jes, we's got done all dat ya ass't. Now, does you have ana'thin' else for us ta do?"

Jes took the opportunity to correct the men's use of the old way of their speaking and to remind all of them, not to call him mister. "I am still just Jes." He asked each one at a time to think about what the teacher, Miss Nan, was teaching them and made them repeat the words one at a time the way she had taught them. Strangely enough, when they had done as Jes asked, each man had a great smile of accomplishment on his face. The greater smile was on Jes's face.

Jes was beginning to wonder about Nan. She was always busy with planning the speaking lessons for the next day and did not mingle with the other women very much. He found her in the room used for teaching, going over the progress that she had made so far. Nan was writing the lessons for their next meeting on a black painted board. She hesitated as Jes voiced his greetings. She started to speak, "Dear friend, and what has you so upset with the biggest frown that I have ever seen on anyone's face."

"Miss. Horton, can I have a few words with you about the mess that our country is getting into?"

Nan looked at Jes and raised a brow.

"It's the coming war Miss Horton. Nan. Mr. Loving and all the hands are concerned about how they will be treated when the Southern armies come marching through our part of the world. It will be a real sad situation for everyone and I am especially concerned about you. I don't think that you have been in the South long enough to really see what the negro-hating white people do to almost all the black people.

"I have a special liking for you and will not stand still if anything should cause you any grief. That's my main concern."

Miss Horton seemed surprised that Jes had made such a statement about any feelings toward her and her cheeks flushed. She finally admitted that she had become caught up with Jes but only in a special friendly way.

"Jes I am honored that you are thinking about my safety should the war come this way but I do not feel that we will see any part of the fighting if it comes to that. Do you think that we will see any Union soldiers marching this far south?"

Jes had no idea just how far the war would affect any part of Alabama but since Georgia was one of the first to announce its sovereignty, there was no telling what might happen to Alabama, so he had to guess.

"Miss Horton, the soldiers that we saw in Woodville on our last visit were getting pretty riled up and making all kinds of angry statements about the damn Yankees, they might just tear the South all to pieces. I hope not but I don't know any more than you do. I am sure that we will find out, and soon.

"Our ranch is not in what may be the main path of the war but I'm sure that it will spread all across the South. The only thing that might help us is that the ranch is located at the far Northwest part of the county and may have only a few soldiers passing through. I hope that will be what happens. I do expect there will be some, maybe small groups, of troops riding through here but not too many We just have to do the best that all of us can to be ready for whatever happens."

Soon was far too soon for all at Mr. Loving's ranch. A week later six horseback riders came onto the ranch and demanded that the ranch turn over all the pigs and at least several steers. The South needs to be fed. They were rag tag and dirty, more like criminals than soldiers.

Jes met them with his double-barreled shotgun under his arm but pointing at the ground. The shotgun was the first thing that the soldiers noticed.

"Hey you damn nigger, what do you think you're doing with that scatter gun?"

Quicker than any one expected, Jes positioned the barrels so that they were still pointing toward the ground but could be quickly raised to point directly at the six mean looking men who claimed to be soldiers. In his best, loud voice, Jes stated he was the protector of Mr. Loving's ranch and intended to do just that, protect and defend everything and anything, "So, get your asses turned around and get going."

All six soldiers turned as gray as their unkempt uniforms but didn't move. Jes deliberately raised his shotgun, pointing it at them. "I won't say this again," and thumbed the two hammers back, ready to fire. "Get your damn asses down the way you came."

There was no doubt that Jes would fire his gun and the men reeled their horses around going back toward Spike and the way that they had come, shouting that they would be back.

Nan and the few black farm hands that were close by stood very still waiting for Jes to explain himself and hopefully give them some plan of what he would do next.

"Sure they will be back and we will not take any demands from such people. If those six men are soldiers, an example of the fighting soldiers that are going to war, it will be a long and dirty war."

1861 and the Ravages of War

For over a month, no gray-clad soldiers rode through the farm. When some did pass by, they seemed always very polite and gave a slight salute doffing their hats as they went by. Unlike the first bums that came to the ranch, these men were dressed in clean uniforms and rode their horses like gentlemen.

Jes guessed that it was about another month when small patrols began to choose the back fields as war grounds. Each time, a group of Northern troops would be hiding in either the cotton or cornfield hunkered down, waiting for the Southern troops to trap them; the shooting would begin and last for several hours with no real gain from either side.

On another day, it would be the Southern troops hiding and lying in wait for the Northern troops. It was a repeat of the same game with the shooting becoming deadly.

Jes had made sure that all the ranch hands were in their houses and laying flat on the floor so that any stray bullets would not find them. The crash of stray bullets was frightening beyond anything that they had ever experienced.

Then the shooting became serious. Larger troops began to arrive and the shooting became deadly.

Jes, with his heart pounding as hard as it could, would take one of the flat bed wagons and collect the dead and wounded. He tried to bandage their wounds the best he and the women of the ranch could. It was very depressing and thankless effort.

When he could, Jes would watch both the Northern and Southern troops ride past the ranch and was very impressed by the way all the horses and men filed past in a parade-like formation, everyone straight in line and the same distance apart. Jes expected no problems from any of them.

All the farm hands were well aware of their coming and slipped out of sight. Jes just stood back in the shadows with the shotgun at the ready. Mr. Loving had warned Jes that he was not to try to defend the ranch because that was his responsibility. He did not want to bring down a full troop of angry men and have them destroy all that they had done. "I want to keep the peace as long as we can" was his only comment to all the hands.

Mr. Loving met the soldiers and shared a few tales of what was happening with the war. They learned that no great battles had been fought nearby but that they were sure to come. One of the very young men expressed that he wanted to see some hard battles and fight like a man. Jes just shook his head and thought that the man was too young to know any better, especially about a dirty, killing war. Jes stopped, thought for a moment, and then added, "Neither do I."

The harvest for the year was not as great as the year before. Both Jes and Mr. Loving blamed the war that had caused some of the fieldwork to slow down. The 1860 harvest was the very best that the farm had ever seen and not everyone thought they would do any better. Great was going to be hard to beat. Mr. Loving expressed his gratitude by having a giant bar-b-cue. Jes did as he usually did and slaughtered the one remaining yearling steer. It was a fine time.

The shadows of the approaching war still hung heavy on everyone's mind and the sound was getting louder and closer with more both blue and gray troops rushing by.

Now, with the war going wild and reports of many soldiers on both sides being slaughtered, the mood of the ranch was sober. Small groups of hands would find a quiet place and ponder what had happened. None could understand what the war was all about.

The landowners in the area where there were white men available to fight, rode off to the war, deserting their plantations, thinking that they would be home in time for the next season's planting. A notice was posted on the Woodville hardware store outside wall, listing the young men from the South killed in the past weeks. The list was getting long.

The dirty community of Spike was not recognized as a place to do any kind of business. The only business that was done in the shambles of Spike was to the few white resettlers. None of the other plantation owners even bothered to go there. It was located so far off a travel direction it was no wonder that the Southern soldiers passed through. It was some six miles to Mr. Loving's ranch from Spike, so they also were not bothered by a lot of traffic.

Over several weeks, different so-called patrols came by the ranch. Mr. Loving and Jes watched very carefully the attitude of each group. It was easy to tell the good guys from the bad guys. The regular Southern troops were always friendly and made no demands of the farm. There were small groups of rag-tag, poorly- dressed gangs of what were called deserters that looked like bums.

In asking the regular Southern troop commanders about the rag-tag bunch, the commanders said that they were mostly Southern, some bad deserters and were wanted by the Southern law and if caught, would be immediately shot. From then on, Jes always stood ready with his pointed shotgun and let them know that regular troops were just over the hill looking for them. Truth or fiction, the bad guys made fast tracks off the ranch.

The war was progressing further south and the sounds of gunfire and at times cannon fire could be heard from the direction of Woodville. When the sounds became constant, Mr. Loving sent a rider into Woodville to learn first hand of the events. He did not trust the so-called grapevine for it had too much misinformation. Mr. Loving always kept his people as well informed as best as he could.

In late 1864, on a very cold day, a battery of four cannons of the Southern troops came charging down the dirt road that went past the farm, over the wooden bridge and to the deserted neighboring plantation. The steel wheels made a loud noise as they traveled across the bridge.

The rebel troops stationed their cannons in front of the out buildings on a flat surface across the stream facing Mr. Loving's farm and made what looked ready to fight. There were four large cannons in the group and several supply carts for the ammunition.

Both Jes and Mr. Loving noticed some of the men had bloody bandages on their heads and at least two had arms in slings. Jes commented that they said that they were in a great bunch of hurt and going on from wherever they came from.

It wasn't long before two Yankee cannons and troops came charging down the same road. It was obvious that they were in pursuit of the rebel troops on the other side of the stream. Like the rebel troops, they also had many wounded wearing bloody bandages on their wounds. The soldiers stopped at the farmhouse and asked Mr. Loving about the rebel battery and the soldiers. Not wanting to lie and cause some angry Yankee soldiers to change their attitudes, Mr. Loving just pointed in the direction of the neighboring plantation and said, "They went that way, just over the bridge."

The Yankee troops were trailing with two more, what looked to Jes and Mr. Loving, heavy bored big cannons, much bigger than the rebel guns. They were drawn by four tired, jumpy-looking horses instead of the usual mules. The horses looked as though they would fall any minute. It was obvious that they had been run hard for many miles.

As the Yankee troops rode near the stream, the soldier in charge turned and pointed to the north, asking Jes, "How would it be if we located our weapons on that hill a few dozen yards from the road, and close to the stream?"

He wanted to place the cannons on the reverse side of a low hill several hundred yards away from the stream. Jes first thought that it was funny to point the guns behind a hill when it looked like the fighting was going to be on the opposite side of the same hill.

"The yanks are just as crazy as the Rebels," moaned Jes.

Jes, not knowing anything about big guns and just where they should be set for firing said that as far as he was concerned it would be just fine. The corn crop had been harvested some days earlier and the cut down stalks were piled in a heap near the south side of the dirt road as they always were so that they could be turned into compost. Jes decided that he could maybe learn something new if he stayed out of the way but had a good look at where the Yankee cannons were going to be placed.

Crow, Jes's favorite mule, had become more of a pest than a working animal. He was in the habit of following Jes every chance that he got. Jes perched himself atop the pile of corn stalks and crow stood close by settling down to observe what was going on. Crow had followed him and was standing quietly behind the stacked corn stalks. They had been settled down for about an hour when from the rebel plantation came a very loud boom.

The Rebels had fired the first shot at the Union troops and it caused a lot of scrambling.

The shot from the Rebel side made a giant uplift of dirt from the eastern direction of the hill but did no damage to the Yankee troops. Jes could see that the Yankee soldiers were not expecting the Rebels to begin firing so soon. It took only a minute or two for the Yankees to respond.

Jes now had his answer as to why the Yankees placed their guns on the far side of the hill. The Rebels guns could not fire over the hill. The first blast from the Yankee guns sent the Rebels scattering. The shell landed short and to the left. The Yankees were already getting their second round ready to fire when another set of Rebel rounds blasted the earth again.

Jes just shook his head. "I hope that they can keep doing just like that for if they keep missing, no one will be killed."

Hardly had he passed on the thought when the Yankees fired a second salvo. The second shot was almost on target. It destroyed one of the Rebel's guns and had to have killed some of the soldiers. Still the Rebel guns began a constant shot after shot at the Yankee position.

They exchanged this type of warfare for over and hour with neither side doing any real damage. Only the one big gun of the Rebel side had been destroyed.

One of the Rebel shots went astray and landed in the center of the dirt road just to the front of Jes and his mule. Jes fell over backwards and the mule was last seen running at a full racehorse gallop, his tail flying straight back. Crow was well aware of the safety of the barn!

Jes scrambled out from the tangle of corn stalks and fell in right behind Crow, his trusted mule. He had learned enough about war and seen enough to satisfy his curiosity about men killing other men.

The events across the stream went on until the next morning when Jes noted that the Rebel guns were silent. He looked at Mr. Loving and said, "Boss, I just have to see if there are any wounded and if so they will need some help."

Jes hurried out to the barn and almost as quick, harnessed one of the horses and hitched it to a flat bed carriage. He wasn't gone long when Mr. Loving noted that Jes was making the horse go as fast as it could. As Jes slid to a stop, Mr. Loving and about half of the hands were waiting for him. In the back of the carriage were three badly wounded Yankee soldiers with blood trickling down their heads.

Without anyone saying anything, hands gently lifted the bodies from the carriage and placed them carefully on the green grass. Quickly as they could, the women assessed the wounds and began to apply bandages. As the ladies struggled with the wounds, streams of tears freely rolled down their weary faces.

Bandages made from torn sheets and other plain bed clothing were placed on the deep gashes of each soldier. Jes said that he had to go back for there were more downed Rebels on the other side and no one was trying to help them. Rube jumped into the carriage with Jes and shouted, "Let's go."

On the east side of the stream there was no place to stop. Jes had the horse running at full gallop when they came to the bridge and did not slow down. Jes thought that someone from the plantation might help but not one person could be seen. The neighboring plantation had been abandoned at the start of the war. There were six badly wounded Rebels lying on the ground with two of them not moving or making any noise.

Jes carefully examined those two first and said to Rube, "These two aren't going anywhere but to their heaven."

Rube asked Jes to give a hand and they lifted the four remaining soldiers into the carriage. Rube hung on to the outside of the carriage, making room for the wounded. It was another dash back to Mr. Loving and the helping hands of Mr. Loving's women.

None of the ranch hands had ever seen a wounded person and were awed when Nan bent down and began to use a regular needle and strong thread to close one of the soldiers gaping wounds. She was talking softly as she inserted the needle again and again until the wound was completely closed. One of the colored ladies joined Nan and began to cleanse and wipe the drying blood from all the wounds.

Mr. Loving stood by and was proud of every one of his people for the way they cared for the wounded and marveled that there was no difference between either the Union and the Confederate troops.

"When a person is badly hurt, it makes no difference what color or which side he might be on," he said to himself. The horrors of war and dying had come to the Loving's ranch. All of the colored and Mr. Loving stayed far into dark dwelling on the tragedy of the day and thinking that the same thing was going on all over the South.

Jes, without asking Mr. Loving, chose one part of the barn for a place to treat the wounded and made it the cleanest that he could. It had been the storage room for all the leather harnesses and had a concrete floor. Wooden workhorses were placed to support the boards where the wounded could be laid for their best comfort.

It was too much for Jes and he wanted to find a quiet place where he could speak to his God.

"Lord what gets into men that they have to kill and destroy that which they have worked so hard to build and own? Is it a sickness or just a mind gone crazy? Forgive me Lord, I am just a poor colored man that doesn't understand. Thank you for listening and hope You do not think poorly of me."

Jes stood back away from the others as he tried to make some sense of it all. In the end, he just bent his head down. "Even though I cannot understand, I have done all that I can and it's up to You, God."

It was late 1863 and at the same time as harvesting. Over the years of the war, the ranch had a number of struggling soldiers from both sides, seeking food and shelter from the ranch and almost always, medical help.

In October, about the 11th, a ragging three, obviously Rebel deserters, came to the ranch and immediately Jes knew that it was trouble. The one that Jes thought was the worst of the three was a short, dirty, stocky-set man that had not bathed in weeks and was the leader. He began to demand in an angry voice, food and some clean clothes.

"No one demands anything from me or the Loving farm. No one."

Things were coming to an end when Nan stepped out of the room she used for teaching. The mean bastard took a different position between Jes and Nan. Jes had stopped keeping the shotgun close at hand and now wondered why. The deserter started toward Nan with the intention to do her harm. Jes bounded for the barn and his shotgun.

A few seconds had passed when he confronted the crazy man. The deserter was not going to drop his desire to get to Nan. He screamed, "Out of the way nigger and drop that scatter gun." When Jes again demanded that the three men leave, the leader of the three was still about to lay his hands on the lady. Jes was not going to allow it. Raising the shotgun and pointing it in the face of the man, Jes let both hammers down and the deserter's head disappeared. The other two fell down on the ground and began to plead not to be shot.

The shock of killing his first person had a devastating effect on all of the hands, and especially Nan. She slumped down folding her hands in her lap, almost screaming, "Please God, Jes didn't mean to kill him."

Jes bent down and took Nan in his arms saying, "I had no other choice. He was determined to harm you and I wasn't about to let that happen. If God thinks that I should be punished, let him go ahead. I would do it all over again if it was the same." He turned toward the two survivors. "You two can take your friend to the white cemetery and dig the grave if you want to. You can place a cross but do not print anything good on the cross, not even his name if you know what it was, for he was a very bad man. Now get going."

Jes bent his head down as the personal disaster at what he had just done overtook his mind and body. He had to find a lonely and quiet place to ask his God for some understanding and forgiveness. The only place that Jes knew was the oak stump behind the barn. He more or less stumbled as he went. For whatever reason his legs just would no longer support him. The stump seemed to welcome him as he crumbled down on the splintered edges and let all his misery flow down his aged cheeks.

"Lord, I just had to kill that mean, dirty, southern piece of trash. He was bent on doing great harm to the one person that I really care about and I just could not let that happen. Please forgive for taking one of your children's lives. I will not do it ever again."

Mr. Loving was in his home when he heard the blast of the shotgun. In a hurry, he shouted, "Jes, what the hell have you done?"

Almost all the colored that were present stepped out in front of Mr. Loving and quickly explained what had happened. Mr. Loving stepped back a step or two and apologized for his abruptness. "I know that you are very protective of everything about the ranch and I have been very concerned that something like this might happen. The deserter got what he deserved and I would have done the same if I had been here."

Everyone watched as the two deserters put the third man over his animal and looking back at the gathering made their way to the white cemetery above the deserted hamlet of Spike.

The pressure on everyone to put the ranch back the way it had been before war started was like a fever. Some of the plows had been without parts and were not used as they should have been, and some were rusty from lack of care. Jes went through each piece and assigned a hand to start to repair where repair was needed. By the end of the first week, most of the work had been done.

The new challenge was putting all the fields that had been neglected also back to where they would sustain the best in crops. Cotton had lost some of it glow as far as export but a new type of seed was about to become available and Jes wanted to look into it, Supposedly, It had longer fiber strands and was much easier to handle for both the harvesting and the end user.

It was late in the evening when a company of Confederate soldiers came riding up to the farm. They were dirty and unwashed. Their uniforms were also torn and no effort had been made to repair them. One had his left arm in a bloody sling. They first rode past the path leading to Mr. Loving's home and then the one that seemed like the leader stopped and looked back. Turning his horse around, he ordered the other soldiers to stand down and then rode back to Mr. Loving's home. In a very polite way, he inquired if he and his soldiers could find a quiet place to rest for the night. Mr. Loving, in the same polite way, directed him to a stand of Oak trees just off the road and near the stream.

"There is a good patch of quality grass for your horses". Then he further stated, "If you care, we would share our food storage with you. Already, most of the chickens and pigs have been confiscated by other soldiers, so why not share what's left with you and your men. It also appears that one of your men is wounded. If you would like, I can have one of my hands look at it and maybe put on new and clean bandages. The stream is clean and cool so you and your men can bathe in the large pool at the edge of the bridge if you want."

Mr. Loving's offer caught the soldier completely off guard and for a moment he had no response. "It is most generous of you. I'll get the wounded soldier and he will be most grateful for some fresh bandages."

Mr. Loving thought that he noted tears slowly forming on the soldier's cheek.

"I can pay you with a supply officer's voucher but I don't know how good it will be when it comes time for you to be paid. But thank you. It is good to be treated in a nice manner for a change. Most of the plantations have also been raided and some of the Union soldiers have laid waste to many of them. It surprises me that your plantation hasn't been destroyed."

Jes had slowly made his presence known and quickly commented, "This ain't a plantation. It's a farm."

There was some contempt on the soldier's face as he wheeled his horse around and joined his soldier friends.

Jes smiled, as he knew that he had rightfully understood that the hands on this farm were not slaves.

It was getting late in the spring for some of the seeds to be put into the ground. Joining Mr. Loving, Jes went over the plans that he had for the beginning of a new season.

"Boss, it's too early for the cotton and about right for corn. Remember the man at the seed place advised us to be strong on the cotton and maybe corn. I do not think that we should plant so much tobacco and no sugar cane. What doe's you think boss?" It was the first time that Jes had reverted to the slang word that he was so concerned to change, "doe's" and he caught Mr. Loving smiling.

"You and most of the hands have done very well since Miss Horton joined us and I think once in a while is acceptable but keep learning."

The ranch was turned almost upside down with mules and men but about every other week, either some Union or Confederate soldiers would ride past the farm with few ever stopping. Some had wounds with bloody bandages showing on their heads and arms in slings. A few would be slumped over in their saddles and others were being aided by their fellow soldiers.

Mr. Loving could not offer any more aid to the ever increasing wounded so he just wished them a safe journey to wherever they were going. There was no spare food and all the cured meat was also gone. Just a few of the smoked cured hams were saved and only because Jes had hidden them under the colored hands beds.

The farm hands that witnessed their passing just shook their heads; for they knew that more had been killed in some far away battle. Their hearts were filled with sorrow and pain for the war was still going on and no one even guessed when it might end.

Several soldiers from the South came by and stopped for fresh water. They seemed to be somewhat lost in their conversations. One especially lingered and talked about the progress of the war.

He let them know that the Union troops had won some of the fighting as far south as Tennessee and that there had been thousands of casualties.

In May of the year 1861, Mr. Lincoln, had issued orders blockading all the seaports in the South and nothing was being shipped. This was a real loss to the Loving farm. Cotton had been praised as the most important product for it was shipped to foreign markets, bringing the greatest profit. With the increased planting of Mr. Loving's fields that would mean a total loss.

When Mr. Loving learned of the situation, he just shrugged his shoulders and stated, "that is the way this crazy war was expected to go and I should have thought about it more seriously." Turning to Jes, he said, "Now what are we going to do?"

Jes was as numb as the boss and followed up with "let me think about that for awhile."

Jes took all afternoon to dwell on the cotton issue. Strolling to the main house, he said that there was just one choice. "Mr. Loving, we have a heavy labor problem when it comes to harvesting the cotton. That is something that we should not do. We can just let the cotton fields go to waste or plow them again and plant hay for the animals or maybe we can sell the hay to either the North or the South. They must have feed for their horses and they do have plenty of them. I just cannot see asking the hands to pick the cotton when everyone knows that it will be worthless. They don't mind the work when it's for a good purpose but hate it when their labor is wasted."

Mr. Loving did as he had done many times, "Jes, you seem to have most of the best answers when it comes to farming. So I want you to do as you stated, plow all the cotton and plant hay."

Jes was heartsick as he stood in the foot tall new cotton plants.

"This is such a waste of seed and man's toil but it must be some one will and pulled up several stalks of the young cotton plants, They have not even grown firm roots yet and I have to destroy all of them," he said to himself.

The cotton stalks had grown firm enough so that they were not easily plowed under. It would take several weeks to turn them under so that they would turn into the desired compost and then into natural fertilizer. Jes chose four of his hardest working hands and assigned them the work of plowing. Much to Jes's dismay, the second plowing did not chop up the stalks as fine as was needed. Taking a handful of the new turned soil, he grunted and directed that a cross plowing was needed. The field, when the cross plowing had been completed, looked like a field for some game. Jes was now ready for the hayseed.

It was late in the month of February 1863 when the ranch learned that Confederate troops had invaded deep into the Union's part of the war front, both in Northern Virginia and Maryland. It was so long ago for the farm, it was not taken with much concern. Jes knew that many more men had died and more would. What did it really prove?

Jes had tried to keep track of how many of both the Northern and Southern men who had been killed. After several attempts, he just gave up.

Mr. Loving and Jes had put off traveling to Huntsville because the charging troops from both sides made any such travel very dangerous.

"Boss, if we don't get some of the new type seeds soon, it will be too late for planting both the corn and tobacco. I don't think that we have to worry about any cotton for it's not worth the seed to plant any."

Mr. Loving agreed. They planned to ride on horseback instead of a carriage for they could travel faster, making the trip in less time.

It was an early Tuesday morning when the two men trotted their best horses down the road and reined them toward Huntsville, Georgia.
With the swift horses, the trip was thought to be over four hours. They slowed to a pace that the horses liked and entered Huntsville in only three

and a half hours and the two men did not feel tired.

The town had seen one of a number of skirmishes with several businesses burned and war damaged.

"Just look at the craziness that war brings," Jes said. "It must have been a nice place to raise families."

They had no idea of where any seed suppliers had their business. Asking street by street, they learned that the only real big seed supply place was on the other side of the town and that's where they headed. Mr. Loving approached a worker and asked about seed availability. The man said that the owner was inside and there was a great shortage of all seeds.

Jes had a slight frown on his wrinkled face and stated to his boss, "I guess that we rode all this way for nothing"

Mr. Loving just as quickly replied, "We need to get acquainted anyway. Our need for the best seed will come from the larger seed companies and I think that the Huntsville Company is much larger than Woodville. It won't hurt to inquire anyway."

The owner was a grizzled old gentleman and had not shaved since the first person set foot on the planet. Struggling up out of his wicker chair, he asked, "Just what can I do for you gentlemen?"

Jes took great note to be included in the use of "gentlemen."

Mr. Loving introduced himself and Jes. "Jes is the field manager of my farm and he and I want to learn something about a new cotton seed that is supposed to be much better than the old standby seed." He went on further telling the owner just where his farm was located and the old man had a slight frown across his aged face.

"Just why do you call your plantation a farm?" the man asked.

Mr. Loving said that he was from England and they didn't keep slaves like they do here in the South. "I have some thirty-seven great colored farm hands and they outwork any slave that I have seen. I treat them as any human should be treated and even pay them a wage for their efforts. It works out just fine and I have great pride in the way they respect each other and me. Jes, here is a good example. He knows more about farming than anyone I have met and he is faithful to the soil."

The man seemed dumbfounded and stared at the two men. "Come on in and let me get acquainted with the only real American that I have met in a long time."

They sat for several hours, learning much about what was happening in the war and about the new seeds that they had only heard about. In the end, Mr. Loving and Jes agreed to purchase a supply of the new seeds when available but they would not be in the warehouse for another month. Mr. Loving ordered them anyway.

The ride back to the farm brought a lot of comment about what they had learned both about the war and farming. Talk about the war disturbed them. From the information that the old man shared with them, it appeared that the war was going very badly for the Confederate armies and maybe, just maybe, the war and all its sadness would be over soon.

Jes had a new gnawing deep in his stomach. There was so much that he didn't know, but wanted to learn, and how were all of them going to do what had to be done to rebuild the Loving farm? We have more to do than I know how to do.

Because the Loving ranch was not in the regular path of the war, so far the war came in bits and sad pieces. Jes tried to keep track of any troops, both the North and South as they passed through.

Sunday breakfast was in the normally quiet eating place, without any idea of troops nearby. The sound of musket fire came from the far northern part of the ranch.

Corn had been planted and harvested. The high drying stalks were all that covered the area fields. Several times in the beginning of the craziness, both sides had used the cornfields as part of their battlegrounds.

What made it so attractive were the many wild pigs and some deer that had made the field and nearby forest their home and shelter.

The wildlife, especially the pigs, made a great food source for either side, and each took advantage of them. The warring troops would kill whatever was available and after dressing them in the field, roast them over a hot open fire to best avoid any detection from either side.

Jes thought it real crazy the way they played the cat and mouse game. Sadly, bowing his head, he commented, "This kind of behavior will ruin the whole country."

On occasion, the hidden troops would catch their enemy, charge out into the corn stalks and fire as many rounds as they dared to do before being fired on themselves.

After the firing, Jes and several of the ranch's hands hitched a flatbed wagon to two of the best mules and would go out into the area of the shooting and, as usual, find and collect the dead and wounded soldiers.

The firing this Sunday morning seemed to be more intense and heavy. Jes knew that they would find more of both sides of soldiers so he asked some of the women hands who had worked as nurses to get as much bandage material as they could find and any pain medicine that they could find and gather in the room that they had already used as a hospital.

Some of the troops from both sides would share their medical supplies, which were very meager, but it helped both the North and South care for the wounded.

It seemed hard for the troops to understand how and why the colored people of the ranch felt a special pain for any soldier that had been wounded.

The dead from either side were reverently buried with a great display of sad feelings and prayers in a special cemetery just above the Spike cemetery. It was in a slight ravine and in the shadows of some old oak trees that had held onto their ragged hanging moss. It was the proper place to put the dead men in their final rest. When they could learn the names of the dead, a wooden marker with the name was added. A solemn prayer with honor was added.

In the search of the cornstalk field and the edge of the woods, Jes came upon a dead soldier of color. Turning him over, Jes recognized the man as his dear friend Rube. Jes was aware that Rube had simply left the Loving ranch and gone north to fight for what he thought to be in the best interest of all colored peoples. Jes fell to his knees, leaned over and lay on the damp ground of the cornfield. The massive pain was unlike anything that he had ever known. The pain was so strong that he was sure that he was dying.

He solemnly lifted Rube, holding him close to his body, and staggered back to the wagon that was being used for all the dead soldiers. He placed Rube's body on the front area to be sure that Rube would get the best attention. There was no feeling in his body and it was a real struggle to lift him into the wagon.

As Jes drove the wagon to the regular colored eating place, many of the hands came out to help with the attending of all the soldiers that were found and killed. A gasp was heard from the crowd as they recognized the body of their friend.

Jes was numb at finding his friend's body. With streams of tears flooding his lined face, he had to find his special old oak stump for thinking and getting himself back to work. All together, they found and put in the wagon eleven wounded and seven dead, both Northern and Southern men. Jes mumbled, what a shame and waste. Jes made sure that Rube was buried under the big oak tree where all the hands who passed away had their final resting place. Every hand on the ranch sang with bowed head, the spiritual songs that they knew Rube most enjoyed.

Jes now had another pain in his heart.

Some had bad wounds in their chests and a surprising number in their upper legs. As soon as a doctor would be available, the leg would be amputated. When Jes learned that a soldier's leg would be removed, he could not help but become sick.

For a few moments, Jes could feel pain in his left leg as though it was being removed. He was more than curious and because he could not explain the feeling, just continued to try to be of some help.

Jes knew that all the hands were troubled by what the war was doing or had done to the ranch. He wasn't sure just what he or any of his friends could do about the problem. In a very slow and troubled walk, he headed to his friend and boss, Mr. Loving.

Mr. Loving gladly asked his number one hand and friend if he would he care for something to drink, anything.

"Just what is bothering you so seriously, Jes?"

As Jes explained his problem, Mr. Loving had a deep frown come over his face. "Jes, dear friend, I've been trying to find some reasonable answer to that very question. Ever since this mad craziness began. In order to save our ranch, one that all of us have worked so hard to establish, I needed to find practical answers but I couldn't find them.

"My sincere prayers seem to be of no avail. I guess our only choice is to do the best that we can do and make very sure that we treat everyone with equal respect and our love. God, how I hope that the North and South can come to their senses soon."

Jes fumbled around with what was on his mind. Finally coughing, he looked Mr. loving straight in the eye. "Boss, we have 19 badly wounded from both North and South. At least 11 have leg wounds so bad I am sure that they will die. I would like to ask you to write a pleading letter to our friend, the man that supplies us with our seeds. He has always asked us about our ranch and offered to help in any way he can. See if he could find us a doctor from either side to come here and take care of all the wounded. He might be able to convince an Army doctor from either side to bring as much medical equipment and supplies as he can get to take care of all of them.

Rube was still in Jes's mind and he momentarily forgot that Rube had been killed while fighting for the North which he believed was in the best interest of all the colored. He had died fighting in the cotton field some time ago. Jes asked one of the other hands to hurry to Huntsville. It's the best and biggest town and should have maybe an extra doctor or Army station with the one person that just might feel sorry for our wounded and come."

Mr. Loving solemnly stated, "Yes, we have to try."

Rube had not even said goodbye when he slipped off and joined the Northern army. Jes found Calvin and gave him the best horse and sent him on his way. As Calvin faded down the dirt road, Jes had a painful feeling of foreboding for the drastic need of a good doctor and the uncertainty of one willing to come to the ranch that he had no idea of.

He trudged back toward the barn, to the teaching room of Nan's school. Nan had taught the hands to emulate the speech of the white man. Jes could not face the crying, screaming and moaning of the wounded soldiers.

The old oak tree stump was calling him as the quietest and best place to do his serious thinking and maybe solve most of his and the ranch's issues.

For some crazy reason the stump was the only place for him to dwell about anything, especially the problems of the ranch. Sitting on the oak wood was the hardest place and contributed to his mood, the war and all the difficulty it was forcing on the ranch. He was doing all that he knew and could do.

He sat for several hours twiddling his thumbs and solving nothing. Finally, briskly standing up, he shook his whole body as to get rid of something of the troubles he was having.

As he walked toward his fellow ranch hands, the colored spiritual crept into his thoughts, "I Ain't Goin' to Have No Trouble No More." It made him chuckle at the thought, because he had more troubles than he thought he'd ever have.

Four days later, Calvin returned from Huntsville with word that he did not find a doctor but the seed merchant had not asked all the medical specialists in the area. He would keep trying.

Jes was disappointed but had expected it. "We just have to pray harder."

Almost a week had passed when a passenger buggy being hard driven by two very sweaty, tired gray horses with two people on board came up the road to the farm.

As the buggy came to a stop, the two people announced that the man was a medical surgeon and that his companion was the hardest working nurse he had ever worked with. As he stepped out of the buggy, he said, "I understand there are a number of badly wounded soldiers here and you need some help. If you can show us where they are, we will do the very best that we know how."

In the luggage box were several large boxes that Jes and Calvin helped unload. The nurse quickly explained that the boxes contained many rolls of bandages. "We collected every one that we could find."

Jes's eyes filled with tears. Within an hour, there was a sharp increase of unbearable screaming and crying.

Jes staggered and stumbled out of the barn where the surgeon was doing his best work. Fear and sorrow spread across his face. All that he could whisper was that they had just cut off a soldier's leg and had no pain medicine to help him. The doctor and his aid worked around the clock for two days. They had lost just five of the most badly wounded thanks to the medical attention of the two people from Huntsville. They had worked tirelessly for two days and one night.

The doctor and his nurse wanted to stay but regrettably had to return to their medical needs in Huntsville. The doctor had expressed that there were hundreds of equally wounded just lying in makeshift hospitals scattered all over the South and few qualified medical people to attend to them. "Many have died and more will die soon. Just as badly as your needs were here, we cannot ignore any of them, but you had no one to give them some kind of hope."

Before they departed, the two medical people rounded up all the ranch women and praised them for the love and medical attention that they had given to the wounded of both sides. It made everyone feel that they had done the right thing.

The doctor selected Alma and made her the leader of the aid for the wounded after they had gone. He again praised her by the way she had paid special attention and the way she took care of the wounded.

As the doctor and his nurse disappeared down the road to Huntsville, Jes stood in the center of the dirt road and silently felt a new pride in being a small part of the human race, colored or white.

Still at a loss of feeling and personal futility, Jes began to wander around all the ranch fields, picking up a handful of soil here, and another there until he had visited every acre of the ranch.

At last, he visited Mr. Loving and explained what he had done. "All of our planting area is in very poor condition, mostly due to neglect during the war years, and will soon need to be put back into the condition of the ranch before the war.

"I'm gathering all the hands tonight and asking them for their help in rebuilding the land, plowing almost all the fields and planting new and maybe different crops. I'm sure that they'll want to see everything like it was back when.

"Boss, I am going to be doing things that we never done before. I'll always tell you, but I want to do them in a hurry and may not always be able to explain them ahead of time. I hope that you will understand and not ask me questions until they are done. We're already late in some of our work."

Mr. Loving, as he usually did, hesitated before answering Jes. "Mr. Jes, I have always been very proud and grateful for all that you have done for our ranch. I don't know how to express my gratitude to you. I will never change.

"If there is ever anything extra, or new, that you want or need, just ask. By the way, what new things?"

Jes was prepared to answer. "Boss, there is more need than we have daylight. Now that full darkness don't come until after nine o'clock, I'm going to have those who will, work until they can't see the ground they're plowing."

Jes had used all his interest and much of his motivation in his meeting with Mr. Loving so that he felt somewhat drained. Now he had to go to his special thinking place, the oak tree stump and think out what he had to discuss and plan for the big meeting tonight with his friends.

One by one in his mind, he reviewed each field and crop to be restored to what the ranch was supposed to be, taking into consideration the most capable man to do the best and timely work.

Word had leaked out about the evening meeting and all hands had decided to honor Jes for taking care of all of them and the ranch. The smoke house had been raided for the last really good ham. Where everything came from was a vague guess. Fire pit roasted sweet potatoes piled high on the serving table, fresh greens were harvested from the individual home gardens and hot, fresh-baked rolls just out of the stone oven thanks to their baker.

Mr. Loving casually strolled down to join the evening. Finally, Jes joined thinking it was the regular evening meal. There was great joy throughout the evening until late into the night.

Jes was out of his house early. It was the last new house that Mr. Loving had planned some years ago. Nan had continued to live in Mr. Loving's house. She and Jes had decided on their own not to be married. Neither wanted the responsibility of raising children.

Even though the South had been defeated, there were still many who felt that they were still Southern rebels and wanted to restart the war.

Jes had muddled through the most important and first-to-be done tasks in rebuilding all the ranch back to its best days. He had been concerned about the best crops, then the best seed and now all of those items had to be considered much later. All the demands came at once and it was starting to overwhelm Jes.

Many of the farming tools were rusted or worn out and no longer usable, and some were even out of date. The repaired old tools had to be checked and put back in shape. Several of the hands were gifted with the forge and fashioned many of the replacement parts so badly needed.

Fresh new animals had already been acquired and all the hands were more than anxious to be back to work. What was next?

Jes didn't have to select which hand to do what. They had already decided that among themselves.

Mr. Loving drew Jes aside and softly whispered, "You should be very proud. Look at what you have done for so many of your, our, people."

Jes selected two of the new mules and hitched them to a duel disc. The disc pulled through good soil would cut about six inches deep, six feet across. The first disc would throw the cut soil to the left and the second trip to the right, turning the soil into a field ready to be furrowed and then planted.

All the hands were overjoyed as they stood at the close of their working day and surveyed what they had done.

Jes had decided that the corn, now in greater demand, be planted first and go in the northern field.

Two weeks before Mr. Loving and Jes had traveled to Huntsville and saw their friend, the seed merchant. The corn seed was a new type and the merchant recommended it because it would yield a bigger crop with better quality. Both men were anxious to get it into the ground.

Mr. Loving asked, "Jes, how much seed of the new kind should we buy?

Jes had the answer on the tip of his tongue and said, "All that we can get. There are several fields we ain't planned for and we can put the new seeds in the ground there."

Over the years, Jes had found his only very private healing place, the old oak stump that was behind the big oak tree and the barn where the colored hands used to go to pray. If anyone ever stepped behind the tree, they would discover the stump. He had found it when he first came to Mr. Loving's ranch. It was his habit to learn every nook and cranny of the ranch and looking in as many of the odd places, he had found the stump.

The war had just ended and the news was stated that everyone could go home. The sadness of learning just how many of both sides had been killed made him want to hide. How could over 600,000 be destroyed and nothing really solved?

Jes mentally tried to measure just what that many lives would look like. Miss Horton was trying to help Jes with numbers and figures, the basic use of arithmetic so he was almost able to understand how many 600,000 represented.

Jes and Mr. Loving sat under the massive oak tree behind the barn and tried to make some sense of what the Loving ranch had paid in terms of destruction of the ranch's assets, food, confiscated animals and the buried, both North and South soldiers. Jes began to count on his fingers how many soldiers of each side they had buried in their cemetery.

River stones were placed around the graves and a wooden marker with the letter "S" for South and the letter "N" for a Northern soldier. Sometimes there was no identity to the pieces of human flesh so a marker that said "unknown" was placed at the head of each unknown.

He shook his head and said, "Mr. Loving, have you ever heard or seen such a waste of people in your life?"

Jes's fingers counted for the South, forty-three men and thirty-one for the Northern men. Both men knew that there had been many, maybe thousands, killed and their graves scattered over everywhere.

Mr. Loving stated that he had never even heard of such a number of killings even during wars in England and France.

"Let's see, as big as Huntsville, no bigger than that. I wonder how big? Where Nan came from? Would it be that big?" Finally, he settled on a whole world full. It had to be that many poor souls gone from the Earth forever. How sad. "I wish that I could have asked her about where she came from."

The other important concerns were the farm. All during the war, from the first day, seeds and any farm parts of equipment were almost impossible to get. All the parts that were made of iron, since the iron was being turned into guns and bullets, there just wasn't any available. One of the ranch hands was a good blacksmith and kept all the horses shod so if iron was available, he was able to fashion new parts that might have worn out or broken.

Still, the ranch had to be rejuvenated and made to grow just as well as before the war. Counting on his fingers, he tried to make sense of all the plows, discs and harnesses into almost like new. He soon ran out of fingers and began to use short sticks as his numbering record.

"I better take a look at all the plows and stuff before I talk to the boss." He gathered up the two farm hands that he trusted with knowing about what was broken and needed fixing. They marched through the places where the farm tools were stored and made a very accurate account. Asking the two to join him, he made for Mr. Loving who was watching for Jes to visit. Although Mr. Loving knew the two men, Jes as a courtesy, introduced them and got a nod of acknowledgement from the boss.

With the assistance of the two farm hands, Leroy and Cal, Jes conveyed all that he had thought of during the day with all three men agreeing to what needed to be done before any effort could be made to rejuvenate the farm. As Mr. Loving had always said to Jes, "You know better what needs to be done. Just tell me what I need to do and all of us will do it."

Jes gathered all the field workers, sitting them down in the eating house. "Today, we're going to walk every foot of Mr. Loving's farm and test the soil, decide just where and what planting will be done and then get to it. Mr. Loving and I will travel to Huntsville and buy the seeds. I know that all the fields have been neglected due to the craziness that now has ended, but it's time to get back to work. We need to find out about the horses and mules, then the harnesses and the equipment that does the real work."

Jes, counting through his mental file, suddenly realized that he had not asked about the hooves of all the work animals.

Turning to Calvin he asked, "Cal? Have we looked at the shoes of all the animals?"

Cal's response didn't surprise Jes for he knew that Cal was especially fond of all the working stock. Cal had only one mule that gave him a bad time. The mule was called Meg and every time she was supposed to get new shoes, she had a bad mule fit. Kicking and screaming in a mule voice one would think that she was being killed. Looking into her face, Cal said that she had a friendly smile to show that she didn't mean it.

"All of the leather harnesses are in good shape. The war didn't require them because they weren't food. We need to check them anyway because some of them may have gone to hell over the years of neglect during the war."

"I just want all of you to know that we have a lot of things that have to be done and that we need to get it done now. Do any of you have something to say?"

As the group of workers broke up and started to do what was needed, Miss Horton quietly slipped into the space. She looked at Jes and asked, "Dear friend, can I have a few moments with you? I want to thank you for what you did on my behalf with that nasty deserter a long time ago. I have tried to meet with you and say thank you but you always seem so busy. Also, I think that you said something that has been bothering me.

"I think that you said that you would not let anything happen to me. Do you remember saying that?"

Jes looking into Nan's lovely face, said, "Yes and I meant every word that I said. I think that you are one special lady to come here and spend a great deal of time trying to knock some white man's language into our heads. I also have some good feelings about you."

Nan was not too quick to reply but when she did, it set Jes back on his heels. "I have been watching you and how you treat all the colored people not only here but when you are around others from the different plantations. I also have noticed how much Mr. Loving depends on you to manage his farm. And Jes, I don't understand why you seem to keep your distance from me. I would like to have a friendly relationship with you if you are interested. I won't bite."

Jes had wanted to avoid such acknowledgement. As he had explained to the boss, "I just don't see how I can have such a person in my life. They always bring children."

Nan must have noticed the thoughts going through Jes's mind. Laying her hand on Jes's arm, "I said I won't bite but I would like to maybe hold your strong hands."

There was no way that Jes was going to move her hand away. Taking Nan's arm he asked her to sit down and let him tell her why.

"I may seem a lot standoffish." He began at the very beginning of how he came to America as a four-year-old-boy and was shoved down into a dark ship's hold. Only because the Captain of the slave ship was human, "I was allowed to be on the top deck. That's how I became just plain 'Jes'." He went on to tell her the whole story of Mr. Loving having selected him at a slave auction.

"I have tried to keep from having a lady friend when I became somewhat jealous of the men and women here who have a togetherness. Now, don't get me wrong, I don't care about bringing any more children into this sad world, especially the way they are treated. That is my real concern. I don't want to be the failing father of colored children because of that."

Nan seemed stunned and didn't even move for many moments. Still she didn't release her hand on Jes's arm. There were small tears slowly escaping down her cheek.

"Dear Jes, it doesn't have to be that way. Even in the North where there are many families of color, a few have, like myself, attended college and become successful at work of their choice. Not everyone can do that. There is as much hate and bigotry there as any place on earth but slowly, people are becoming more understanding about us people of a different color.

"I think that you will never want to leave Mr. Loving's and this farm and you shouldn't have to. We don't have to be married and grow a family but it would be nice to have someone to love."

There it was the magic word, "love." Jes had never felt that he could love anyone the way that she would want to be loved. What was he going to do now? Down deep in his heart, there was a feeling about Nan that he had never known. Was this the meaning, thoughts and feelings that everyone was involved with? Just what was he going to do about it, and with the special lady sitting next to him? He had to do something.

With a loss for words, Jes leaned back from the bench and looked at Nan for some time. He was trying to learn just what the lady was seeking. Did she want to be just good friends or was she searching for a mate and marriage? He couldn't make any sense of her posture but the questions were obvious, she needed some level of serious friendship.

Jes had hesitated too long, for Nan put more pressure on his arm and asked, "Am I causing you to become frightened?" She continued to press

Jes's arm. "How about you and I just walking along life's path for awhile and seeing if we like each other?" She slowly released his arm.

Jes didn't want to let Nan's close contact stop. Lowering his head like a bashful kid, he slowly began by selecting his words very carefully, just the way Nan had shown him.

"Dear lady, I do not have very much experience with women that I think a great deal of. I do not know how to treat such a person. A long time ago when I was about twelve or thirteen, one of the older ladies at a plantation that I have forgotten the name of, scared the devil out of me by taking me out into some woods and doing what women do to men. I was just a boy at the time and had no idea what I should do. She taught me and I cannot say that I did not enjoy the experience. She continued to have me join her in the woods several more times. Each time I had a guilty feeling that we were doing something wrong.

"Over the years, seeing how many of the people of color manage their personal lives and get together in a very friendly way, I remember the days in the woods and get a little lost. I have no idea what you would like me to be in your life but I do want to share whatever it is with you."

Nan had a devilish smile all over her face. "That, dear friend, is all that I ask right now. I will be as slow with your personal lessons as I have been with your learning the proper way to speak. Now let's go for a walk, and not in some woods." Hand in hand, they trudged away from the main part of the ranch, walking through the shoots of new sprouting corn and on to the far field next to the woods. Here, they found an old log that offered them a sitting place.

Nan began to try to delve into Jes's thinking ways. She began by asking about his experience with the older lady in the woods a long time ago, all the time holding his hand and trying to feel his emotions. He explained that he was too much of a private person that Nan could not feel any of his reaction and gave up. Ending the walk in the far fields and taking time out to rest on the old log

Still holding hands, they took the shortest way back to their family group.

Mr. Loving noticed that Jes had a smarter step in his way of walking and cornered him to find out what had changed. After Jes explained to him truthfully, Mr. Loving gently said, "I was sure that it was something to do with the teacher and it pleases me. She also has a friendlier attitude lately. "You are remembering the farm work aren't you?"

Jes seemed shaken. "Boss, the farm is my whole life. How could you even think that I'd neglect any part of it? We're about ready to start the spring planting and as you know, the tobacco is planted first and then cotton:"

Mr. Loving stopped Jes and let him know that he was well aware of the different planting procedures. He then reminded Jes that they did not have some of the new type seed for the cotton. "We need to visit Huntsville again.

"We have to replace almost all the farm animals, especially the working horses and mules. The soldiers from both sides took the food animals, even the old mules that had to be too tough to chew for their food.

Mr. loving interrupted and said that he had dispatched a letter to his legal friend asking for help in finding the best both horses and fine mules, especially ones with calm tempers. He stated that they would have his legal persons help when they got to Huntsville.

When everyone learned about a trip to Huntsville, Nan insisted that she be included. "I need to purchase new and different material. Some of my students are beginning to learn to write and spell basic words and I want to have the latest books and writing material. About half of the hands are putting in a lot of night studies and Jes is one of them."

Much of the South failed to recognize that the Civil War was over and that the South, the Confederate states, had lost. The flags of the Rebels were flying over all the main business stores and shops. Mr. Loving, Nan and Jes directed their carriage through town toward the warehouse of the seed merchant. The ugly remarks coming from many still clad Southern soldiers were very abusive and in many cases, vulgar. Both Jes and Nan looked straight ahead and hoped that their stares would send the message that the street noise was just the poor way of trying to insult them and maybe draw some response that would give the Rebels means to really get ugly.

As they tied the reins of the animals to the hitching post, the same grizzly old man stepped out from under the overhangs and greeted them like long lost friends. "I've been expecting you two but not with such a pretty lady. Are you here for the best seeds in the South? Step right down and let me serve you some real cool cider."

Jes quickly informed the seed merchant that they had to meet Mr. Loving's legal attorney for assistance in buying replacement animals taken during the war.

I know of Mr. Goldman and he is one fine gentleman, so they say. He is one of the good things that the war brought to our part of the country. Everything is still in one hell of a mess. The southern people won't admit that they have lost the war and cling to the attitude that the South will rise again. Not a chance.

Mr. Goldman had received Mr. Loving's letter and had contacted several animal dealers and found that there were many fine animals to be bought. He had taken the liberty to close a deal on ten fine well-trained plow horses and an equal number of not-too-feisty mules. Getting them to the leading rack would be Jes's problem.

The 1866 season was at hand and the farm had never looked more ready to plant. The trip to Huntsville had renewed the friendly meeting of the seed merchant and he was eager to hear about what had happened at the Loving ranch. He still got a tickle when he said "ranch". "I have shared that saying with many of my other seed buyers and they all would not believe it. I promised some of them that the next time you two came to town, I would ask if you would be willing to have a talk with them. I don't want to push but you would be doing me a great service to tell them straight out about how you pay for your colored farm hands. No one around here would think of such an operation. Most still have the belief that the South did not lose the war. They will be rebels until they die."

Planting started the day after Jes and Mr. Loving returned to the ranch.

Jes met Nan and they both stared out over the cornfield and couldn't believe what was going on. Every colored hand was row by row placing the seeds by hand. Jes called one of the men out. "How come you're planting by hand?"

He responded, "We're just doing what you do, talking to each seed that we put in the ground. If you get better crops than we do then all of us will say we should try your trick. Besides we save a great many of that seeds because only they one's that goes in the soil sprout and become a crop. Is that okay with you?"

Nan watched the expression on Jes's face. She wanted to learn as much about this tall, fine, good-looking man that she had become fond of. Nan asked, "Dear Jes, just why do you talk to the seeds anyway?"

Jes had to think about how he should answer her question. "Lady, it's a personal thing with me. I'm so fond of all the work that we do, I find if I ask questions of the different items, they do better. I know it sounds crazy but it makes me feel good and that's all that matters."

The worker responded, "I don't trust the new planter that you brought back from the town and anyway, we want to make sure that the right number of seeds gets into the proper place in the ground."

As the two looked on, Jes said, "That's the best picture any one could ever see. Happy people of color singing their special spiritual songs and letting the troubles of the world just go by. It makes one proud to be alive."

Nan took his arm and led him to the edge of the field where the planting was going on. "We need to have a serious talk, dear friend.

"I have thought much about your wants for your future and tried to understand where I might be a part of your life. Like you, I have no real desire to bring new life into this very biased world and have them struggle as both of us have done. I do want to become close to you but don't know how. Have you any plans or suggestions how we can live together?"

"Mr. Loving has a very strict rule about anyone living together and not being husband and wife. I am sure he wouldn't think good of us doing what you suggested. I know that he's aware of our caring for each other but that doesn't matter when it comes to living together and not being married. The best that I can suggest is that both of us must ask him what would be fine with him due to the fact that no family is planned. What do you feel about that?"

"If that's the best way, let's see what he will say."

Mr. Loving was sitting on his front porch having one of the few refreshments that had alcohol as one of the main ingredients. He had become very fond of the local mint juleps and favored several at the close of each day. He was a little surprised when two of his favorite people came strolling along the path from the front of his home. His first sight was them holding hands.

Mr. Loving greeted them as one would very important friends.

"I guess you two have something important to say. Nan, you look the bright shining flower that you are. Now tell me what you have on your minds."

Jes first looked at Nan, expecting her to speak. She in turn, looked Jes straight in the face with a little strength in her voice, "Jes, this is your idea so go ahead and tell him what's bothering us. Well not bothering, but concerns both of us."

"Boss," Jes began, "it's no secret that Nan and I think a great deal of each other and have decided to try and make a home together. We both know of your rule about unmarried couples living together. We've talked a lot about being together and not worrying about having children. There are enough children about that should we need their love, we can just borrow one or two. We're asking how we can abide by your rule and have a home of our own."

Mr. Loving had been well aware of the two for some time and had thought how he was going to solve the issue for them.

"Jes, it's 1881 now. How long have we been together? I think that you first came to the ranch in 1844. That seems like a long time ago. I believe that adds up to some thirty-seven great years. Nan, isn't that correct?

"We've made this ranch into more than I had ever dreamed of and most of that is because of your hard work and devotion to me and the soil. I've been thinking how I could say how much I appreciate all that you and all the colored hands have done to make that happen. I've had a surveyor mark off the 200 acres that is on the South side of the road and next to the stream that separates my ranch from the neighbor's plantation. He has recorded the property in my name and deeded it to you with full ownership.

"To answer your and Nan's question, let it be a wedding from a true friend and you have my sincerest blessings but with one request. When you two get married, and you will be married, I want to give the bride away and hold the dandiest feast that anyone in the county has ever seen. Now, is there anything that I may have forgotten?

"There are some stipulations that you have to abide by and they are simple. You must continue to manage the ranch just as you have in the past, taking care of your property as you go along. Gosh, this makes me feel good."

Both Nan and Jes sat still, feeling numb. What had just transpired was nowhere in their plans. They thought that Nan would move into the home of Jes and she would make it into a woman's home with fine curtains, some extra closets and maybe nice, proper rugs on the floors. It was more than both people could stand and tears began to make running streaks down both their cheeks. Their legs were like stone and neither could stand up and walk. Finally, Jes took Nan's hand and struggled to his feet.

"Come on dear lady, we have a great deal to think about and plan."

Mr. Loving quickly said, "Just sit still for a moment. I haven't finished what I want to say. I'm getting along in age and know that I cannot attend to all that needs to be looked after. So, Jes, I want you to begin to take complete charge of everything on the ranch and treat it as your own. I am sure you understand what it all means.

"I'm also sure that the men and women of color will want to continue to be a part of the goings on for I have quietly asked all of them and they assured me as long as they're treated the same as they've been treated, they don't not want to go to any other place. As you know, I set up bank accounts for each of them and deposited their earnings in the bank. I'll continue to pay them as always and will show you how I arranged all of it."

It was mid-May when Jes knew that a change was coming.

Mr. Loving called Jes to his home and sat him down, along with a person that Jes had never met. Mr. Loving quickly introduced him as a legal person of great knowledge.

"I've asked you and this gentleman to arrange for me my final request for the care of our ranch. Jes, you have shared with me so many good, no, great times that I know you'll abide with what I have to do to protect all of the hands and especially you and Nan.

"His name is Goldman and as I earlier stated, one of the best legal people that I know of. He has taken down all of what I want as a binding trust for the management of the ranch and you are to be the administrator and carry out all my wishes. I know that you can do as I've requested and make sure all the ranch hands are well taken care of.

"Mr. Goldman will work with you to make sure that everyone complies with my wishes, for there are scalawags who will try and cheat you out of this ranch that we have worked so hard to make one of the best in the state. It's a lot of legal stuff that you don't need to be bothered with unless someone tries to lay some kind of claim on the ranch. Mr. Goldman will see to it that no one will have any success.

"Do you have any questions? Jes, I owe this to you for all that you've done for me and all the colored people of the ranch."

Jes was completely without any words. He was well aware that his friend was in failing health at the age of eighty-one. It had to be expected for anyone who had put so much into his dream. Jes sat very still until Mr. Goldman asked if Jes understood what Mr. Loving had said.

Finally, Jes stood up and faced Mr. Loving. "I know that you're coming to the end of your time, just as I am. I haven't given any thought about my time left on this earth. I may have a few more years remaining. I will do exactly as your directions say, and Mr. Goldman, I need to tell all this to Nan and get her to help me remember what has to be done." Jes just quickly explained to Mr. Goldman who Nan was. "She's my keeper, my heart and educator."

The three men continued sharing the afternoon and some of Mr. Loving's cooks fine cake.

Jes was at a complete loss at what he had just learned. On his worn and craggy fingers, he began to count the years and times that he had been the field boss of some 40, and, at times, 47 devoted ranch hands. Now all of a sudden, they were his responsibility. The thought of being responsible for the lives of anyone scared the devil out of him. Now that it had happened, he simply said to himself, "I can do that."

It was the middle of July 1874, on a bright clear day, when the older housemaid of Mr. Loving came staggering to Jes with tears flooding down her face. "

Mr. Jes," She had never called him mister before and it sent a cold chill down Jes's whole body.

Slowly, she said that during the night, Mr. Loving just went to sleep. "I didn't hear anything but this morning when I went to take his coffee, he was lying like he was asleep but had no breath coming out of him. You have to come quickly now Mr. Jes and tell us what to do."

Even though Jes knew his friend and boss had very little time remaining, he was deeply saddened and somewhat surprised at the maid's news. Kind of stumbling along, he went to tell Nan and get her help in telling all the hands that he was now responsible for their best interest and welfare.

With everyone gathered in the main eating place, Jes addressed them, with tears running in a crisscrossed river down his craggy face. The word of Mr. Loving's passing had preceded him and there was nothing but pain showing on all the down-turned faces. Still Jes had to assure all of them that Mr. Loving had made legal plans for everyone and that nothing would change.

"We all have worked long and hard to make this ranch the dream of our now departed friend and it is my responsibility to see that it continues just like in the past.

"Mr. Loving planned way ahead and wanted his remains to be set in the soil on the knoll under the oak trees where the past war first came to the ranch. All of you know just where that is. There are some Rebel and Yankee men also resting there so he'll be in great company. As soon as Leroy and the other carpenters can fashion a proper coffin, we'll have his remains set in the soil that he treasured so much."

Jes watched all the rest of the day and far into the night as Leroy and his best men used the stronger oak wood to finish a fine coffin. They had polished the wood so that the grain of the oak stood out like rivers of dark earth.

When it was completed, Jes gave the praise of how wonderful it looked. Leroy then added, "The dark is like the color of our skin. I wanted to leave something that said that all us colored were most honored and proud to be a part of his ranch. That man never had a bad word for any of us and I never heard him call us anything but ranch hands. I don't know how we became so lucky to be treated so kindly."

All the men stood around the dark object for many minutes before Jes commented.

"Dear friends, come let's not linger here any more. The women are preparing the body and tomorrow we'll do what has to be done with everyone sharing this sad time."

Jes and all the ranch hands agreed that Mr. Loving's body would be interred at noonday while the sun was directly overhead. Some of the men who weren't involved in the coffin making had selected the best spot under that big oak tree that had stood on the knoll for many years. Fresh sod had been laid aside to cover the new dug earth. As everyone gathered for the final burial to take place, most of the farm hands began to sing some of their most treasured spiritual songs. "Going Home," "Ain't Going to Tarry Here," and "Nobody Knows the Trouble I've Seen."

A granite headstone was planned to mark the grave. Jes asked Nan to write the words that he wanted carved in the stone. It was all that anyone could do.

As they neared their homes, the bass singer of the group, with resounding tones, sang the last course of "Peace in the Valley," which echoed across the ranch.

"No headaches or trouble or misunderstanding. No confusion or trouble — won't be no frowns, just a big endless smile. There'll be peace and contentment for me."

The rich tone of the voices continued all the way to their homes. Jes had never felt so proud of his life with Mr. Loving and these wonderful trusted friends.

The voices sounded far across the fields that had been the working places of all the hands for many years. Slowly, after the grave was closed, in a single line, they marched back to the main eating place and sat quietly until Jes stood up and reverently said, "Lord, we will miss our master, He did not ever want to hear us call him master but he did so much for all of us, it would be disrespectful not to give him the praise of making all of us feel above slavery. Be very gentle with his soul, dear Lord, for he was a very good man."

Jes had not made any special arrangement for food but again, the reason for celebration of a man that they all loved required such a feast, Leroy and one other of the hands had planned a regular, but special, feast. Several others had slaughtered a choice pig and it had been slowly roasting over the spit for hours. Roasted sweet corn, sweet potatoes and sweet potato pies were ready for everyone to enjoy.

Jes had never really had what he called "family members" together in one place at one time and as he looked around, he slowly counted them. Taking Nan by the hand and looking into her pretty face, he smiled, grateful.

"Dear lady, this is now our family. We have to do what Mr. Loving would do for all of them. I'm not sure just what I have to do but with you beside me, it shouldn't be too hard."

No one said a word but the roasted pig was set out on a table. Several of the men began to slice generous portions from the dark brown meat, so tender that it fell from the bone.

Months had passed when Jes noted that Nan's way of doing everything had slowed somewhat. "Let's walk over to our most treasured place, I want to ask you some important questions."

Jes had never approached Nan in such a manner and she stood up asking, "Dear love, is there something I've done that disturbs you?"

Jes had never failed to respond to Nan in any other way but the facts and truth.

"Dear woman, I have noticed that you aren't yourself lately. Is there something wrong that I should know about?"

Nan's head dropped slightly and she began to speak very softly.

"My dearest and most special friend. You are very observant. I have been avoiding telling you but I'm having some kind of health problem. I seem to have lost much of my willingness and strength. It's been very difficult to just move about for the past two months. I have no idea what is wrong but something has happened."

Jes had never thought about being white, but he felt that his skin had turned dead white at what Nan had just shared with him. He sat for a longer period than he had ever done before. Then in a strong voice, "We'll have to go to the best doctor that we can find. There are no such medical people, even in Huntsville, so that will mean a trip to Tennessee and good doctors."

It took Jes two days to learn of the best medical service anywhere close by. He had never ridden a train but getting tickets for two colored people became a challenge. Finally, with the help of Mr. Goldman, he and Nan would spend a full day getting to the city of Nashville.

Their troubles had just begun. They were ordered to sit in a special section with signs clearly displaying, "colored people only." The personnel of the train just glared at them as they sat very quietly. Nan had put together a small lunch of several sandwiches and a bottle of clean water. They found that they couldn't buy any of the train's food or water. Nothing had changed in the South concerning the attitude of the end of slavery.

In Nashville, they quickly found a white doctor that took special care of colored people and welcomed Jes and Nan to his office. It was two days of intense poking, feeling and testing when the doctor finally informed both Jes and Nan that Nan had a failing heart.

Even with the best medicine, there was nothing that could be done for Nan.

As a special period, Jes insisted that they walk around that town of Nashville and enjoy some of what the big city had to offer. Jes bought several clothing items for Nan and found an eating place that served the colored people. After walking around Nashville for several hours, both were surprised and said that they didn't want any part of a big city.

This is why I was glad to leave the big city of Chicago," Nan said. I don't miss it even a little bit."

The train ride back to Huntsville was a somber one. Jes held Nan's hand so tightly that several times she had to ask him to let go.

Nan finally turning to her man, "Jes, promise me that you'll have me buried as close to Mr. Loving as you can. I know that you have several places reserved for someone and I want to ask you for the one that you favor the most. Promise me."

With a renewed flow of stain-making tears flooding his weathered face, Jes bent low and kissed her softly on both cheeks. "Dear lady, you did not have to ask me, I had planned to do just that, saving the other one for myself."

Jes couldn't get past the sick feeling deep in his stomach and found it impossible to have meaningful conversation with Nan, who sat staring out the window wordlessly. It was a very difficult time for both of them. Nan took Jes's hand and he noticed that there was a trembling and stiffness in her touch.

Back at their home on the Loving ranch, the news about Nan was taken as hard as the passing of Mr. Loving.

For whatever reason, Nan went to meet her God in two months. She had been such a strong influence to all the ranch hands that for four days and nights, they sat moaning in the eating shelter. The spiritual songs that Nan loved to listen to were repeated over and over with the singing people saying that they wanted to make sure she could hear them all the way to her heaven.

Many of the neighboring colored people came to say their good-byes. The best colored spiritual songs filled the evening services. There was nothing but the kindest and most loving words spoken about Nan.

Jes crept off behind the giant oak tree behind the barn where he and Nan had spent many hours planning their future. He renewed as many of the moments as he could remember.

It was near sunset of the fourth day when Jes finally joined the Loving ranch hands and thanked them for such a wonderful goodbye for his Nan.

For several long, lonely months, Jes could barely get the work done. He seemed to stagger from one task to the other. Finally, sitting down on the always-stacked pile of corn stalks, he began to talk to himself.

"Jes, you old black man, you been a slave on many plantations and done well. You was found by one of the best men I will ever know, Mr. Robert Loving, from a place called England where they treat all people with equal respect. He made you his ranch manager and gave you pay for doing what you always wanted to do. He brought Miss Horton to the ranch to teach colored people how to speak proper English like the white man. Nan became my caregiver and love, which I never thought I would find.

"Now, just what is wrong with you?" With the most solemn emotion Jes had ever felt, he promised his late Nan that he would do much better for her.

Jes's usual special place to reflect on anything was the giant oak stump and tree behind the barn. Lately, there was no solace and comfort under the giant tree. He found that so many wonderful moments had been spent with Nan and Mr. Loving using the tree as a place of good feelings that nothing was like that anymore. He just wandered across the big fields that he and all the hands cared so much for, talking aloud and kicking up a clod of soil as he went.

There were the most heartbreaking emotions in his stride as he passed several fields of growing seeds. He had to find a place where nothing but his own grief could be considered. He and his faithful, friendly mule wandered to the stream crossing that separated the Loving ranch from the now abundant neighboring plantation. The leftovers of corn stalks had been piled next to the stream on the Loving side and Jes had many times sat on the pile and observed the acres of growing corn and cotton and felt great pride.

For whatever reason now, he found that the corn pile was his private shelter from all the troubles that had overcome him. Almost every day at the end of work, he would be drawn to the one place to recall his best memory of Mr. Richard Loving and his love, Nan.

He knew that most of his thoughts were in his emotions and imagination and that made it more pleasant and not so real. He had been using the corn stalks as a refuge for almost six years. The sound of the flowing stream added to the pleasant surroundings that meant more to Jes than anything. He and his mule would mosey to the stalks around early evening and just wait quietly for darkness to fall and to join his fellow ranch hands.

Jes had been so caught up with the loss of Nan and trying to keep the ranch running as it should, he didn't give the proper last goodbye to his faithful animal, Jack. Now, bowing his head he said a short prayer just for Jack. Jack had lain down in his stall and gone to meet his God.

The hands always knew what was happening with their leader and friend, Jes. They respected his quiet attitude and gave him all the space for his private moments that he needed.

Jes wasn't feeling his best in late September of 1884 and was very much aware that his time on earth was coming to an end. His bones pained him constantly and his memory was becoming very difficult to recall. His emotional thoughts were mostly of seeing Nan in his afterlife. He still didn't have a strong belief in the God that almost all the believers spoke of as a real person. He trusted the God that had always been a strong part of his heart.

Now with time being short, he dwelled a lot on his feelings of heart as the goodness of man and the closeness of all his people. As he sat deep in the corn stalk pile, his mind first thought that he was hearing far off, a song that he was sure was meant for him. At first because the sound was so far away, he couldn't make out the words. As they became closer, he was sure that the voice was that of his long ago friend, Rube, who had been killed in the war by the Southern soldiers and laid to rest on the hill near Mr. Loving and his Nan. It was a long time before he could clearly understand the words.

Turning his head for a better and clearer sound of the voice, he was sure that he clearly understood.

"I'm coming, I'm coming, for my head is bending low,
I hear the gentle voices crying, Old black…

He knew the last word was Joe, but he was Jes.
I'm coming, I'm coming, but I am just Jes

Conclusion

Although Jes is pure fiction, Jes wouldn't be complete without coming to a final end.

I Am Just Plain Jes.

Somewhere about 30 miles southwest of Woodville, Georgia is a great ranch. Along the west side of the ranch is a clean, clear stream and near the stream is a beautiful knoll with a solitary giant old oak tree with streamers of gray hanging moss.

At the base of the knoll, there are some 40 grave markers with a single letter carved deep into the marker. One with a letter "N" and another the letter "S" — "N" for North and "S" for South. Buried beneath each marker is a Civil War soldier who paid the ultimate price for his belief in country.

Further up the slope is a carefully cared for group of markers, each with just one name carved in large letters. The names are of the original colored hands that had worked the ranch not as slaves but as hired hands.

Just barely under the shady side of the old oak tree, near the top of the knoll, these names are carved in the gray stones: R. LOVING, N. HORTON, RUBE, CALVIN, and a little farther along, ALMA.

Above all these is one solitary marker that bears the words "JUST Jes".

References and Notes on Speech

Most of the so-called African to English words were found in the research for JES. The list is just a small part of the many pages on which I found any explanation of the words people used to use.

Research documents:

1) My Folks Don't Want Me to Talk About Slavery, edited by Belinda Hurmence. Published by John F. Blair.

2) The Sounds of Slavery, Shane White and Graham White. Beacon Press, Boston.

3) Negro Folks Expression, Sterling Brown.

Additional,
Life of Ashland B. Helen, plantation.
Emancipation Proclamation
Slave Plantation
Plantation system
Slavery in US
Louisiana Plantation
Radical Republicans
Underground railroad American Civil War.
and many other references.

Art Barnes

Black English

One theory holds that the slaves' variety of English developed from a pidgin that resulted from the conditions of the slave trade, which brought together speakers of different African languages and forced them to communicate through a pidgin language. This pidgin was used by slave traders and slave owners to communicate with blacks, and by blacks of different linguistic backgrounds to communicate with each other. Out of this developed a Black English creole spoken by the first generations of slaves born in North America.

This creole can be heard today spoken by the Gullah and Geechee inhabitants of the Carolina Sea Islands. Another view holds that Black English results from the retention of British English features that have not been retained in other varieties of American English.

This speech is characterized by pronunciations (phonology), syntactic patterns (grammar), and morphological features (inflections). Many of these features are shared by Southern white speakers and by Appalachian speakers. The features below represent tendencies toward these speech patterns.

Samples of this include:

door— [do:] "doah"
sister—"sistah"
help —"hep"
steal — "steah"
ball — "bah"
you'll — "youah"*
they'll —"deyah"/"dey"
passed — "pass
good man — "goo´ man"
like — "lak"
time — "tam"

why — "wha"
they — "dey"
them — "dem"
think — "tink"
thin — "tin"
three — "free"
throat — "froat"
nothing — "nuffin'"
brother — "bruvvah"
tenth — "tenf"/"tent"
mouth — "mouf"/"mout"

In JES, the author attempted to use a smattering of these speech patterns to give the reader a feel for the manner of speaking of the time.

no more — no mo'	the — de
poor — po	they — dey
your — to	don't — do'n
hands — hans	there's — dars
shut — shet	cold — col
just — jus	first — fus
every — ebery	this —dis
folks — foks	with —wid
soft — sof	because — cus's

www.ingramcontent.com/pod-product-compliance
Lightning Source LLC
Chambersburg PA
CBHW070822020826
48982CB00014B/169

* 9 7 8 1 6 0 4 1 4 8 1 1 4 *